AA58   N52   SCI

E222   IO4   R...

P25   H...

JAS

RT13   RT35   ST 32

DEEP SOUTH DOCS!

Swapping the Big City...for the Bayou!

When two delectable doctors arrive
in America's Deep South, looking for a
fresh start, they soon find themselves
falling for the charm of Bayou life—
as well as for the attractions of the
beautiful women they're working with!

But big-city surgeons with their bright
ideas aren't always welcome in the Bayou.
Especially when they're super-hot,
heart-stopping distractions for the dedicated
Deep South nurses. These women have
enough complications as it is, without
falling for the new docs in town...!

**The first story
in Dianne Drake's *Deep South Docs* duet
A HOME FOR THE HOT-SHOT DOC
is also available this month from
Mills & Boon® Medical Romance™**

Dear Reader

When I went to Louisiana for the first time a few years ago—specifically New Orleans, and all the deep, dark backwoods of the bayou surrounding it—I knew I wanted to set a book there. It's a beautiful place, and there's nothing else quite like it in the United States. In fact, descriptions don't do it justice…but I've tried in this duet titled *Deep South Docs*.

Both stories, A HOME FOR THE HOT-SHOT DOC and THE DOCTOR'S CONFESSION, centre around the Doucet family and their daughters, all of whom work in the medical field in some capacity. In this duet you'll meet Mellette, who has to overcome one of life's greatest tragedies in order to find true love again. And you'll also meet Magnolia, who just can't seem to find time for love in her life.

Both meet men who try to capture their hearts, but it's not an easy thing to do as the Doucet family is filled with eight mighty strong women and one man who sits at the head of it and who's the biggest softie in the world. But, as both Justin Bergeron and Alain Lalonde discover, the fight is worth the effort…most of the time. At other times Mellette and Maggie are almost too much to handle.

When I was taking a boat ride through the swamps in the Louisiana bayou, perhaps the thing that fascinated me most were these little communities of people who live out there in the swamp, almost totally cut off from society. I could see the shacks almost everywhere. In fact we even took a detour by our tour guide's shack and saw a whole lot of alligators lounging in his front yard. He said that as long as he didn't bother them, they didn't bother him. Well, I don't know about that, but it certainly made for an interesting trip. So did the alligators that would swim right up to the boat.

I hope you enjoy your trip to the Louisiana bayous. It's fascinating. And after *this* trip to the bayous I'm going to hang around to write a few more books based in that part of the world, so look for Sabine and Delphine's stories coming next.

I like to hear from my readers, so please feel free to contact me at diannedrake@earthlink.net, or visit my website page at www.dianne-drake.com, from which you can link to either my Facebook page or my Twitter page.

As always, wishing you health & happiness

DD

A DOCTOR'S CONFESSION

BY
DIANNE DRAKE

First published in Great Britain 2014
by Mills & Boon, an imprint of Harlequin (UK) Limited,
Large Print edition 2015
Eton House, 18-24 Paradise Road,
Richmond, Surrey, TW9 1SR

© 2014 Dianne Despain

ISBN: 978-0-263-25453-2

Printed and bound in Great Britain
by CPI Antony Rowe, Chippenham, Wiltshire

Now that her children have left home, **Dianne Drake** is finally finding the time to do some of the things she adores—gardening, cooking, reading, shopping for antiques. Her absolute passion in life, however, is adopting abandoned and abused animals. Right now Dianne and her husband Joel have a little menagerie of three dogs and two cats, but that's always subject to change. A former symphony orchestra member, Dianne now attends the symphony as a spectator several times a month and, when time permits, takes in an occasional football, basketball or hockey game.

Recent titles by Dianne Drake:

A CHILD TO HEAL THEIR HEARTS
P.S. YOU'RE A DADDY
REVEALING THE REAL DR ROBINSON
THE DOCTOR'S LOST-AND-FOUND HEART
NO. 1 DAD IN TEXAS
THE RUNAWAY NURSE
FIREFIGHTER WITH A FROZEN HEART
THE DOCTOR'S REASON TO STAY**
FROM BROODING BOSS TO ADORING DAD
THE BABY WHO STOLE THE DOCTOR'S HEART*

**New York Hospital Heartthrobs*
Mountain Village Hospital

CHAPTER ONE

"HE'S HANDSOME ENOUGH," Magnolia Loraine Doucet—Maggie—commented. It was one of those hot, hot August days in Big Swamp, where her preference was to sit on the front porch swing, fan herself and sip a tall, cool lemonade. Which was exactly what she was doing with her sister Mellette on the front porch of Eula's House.

Inside, Mellette's husband, Justin, was arguing with Amos Picou on just how much larger the clinic extension should be. Amos wanted to keep everything as it was, and Justin wanted things bigger—a surgery for minor procedures, a cubbyhole where he could escape to write pages for his latest crime novel. It wasn't a lot in terms of square feet, but changes were met with resistance in these parts.

And while the argument with Amos, who was in favor of leaving things be, was not nearly as heated as the noonday sun, it had seemed the perfect time for the sisters to go outside and take a break.

"You mean drop-dead-gorgeous carpenter man without his shirt, and all sweaty. And look at his…" Mellette Bergeron teased.

"You're a pregnant lady with a husband just inside the door. You don't get to look at his anything."

"Hey, I can still look…a little."

"You've got a looker. Got him hook, line and six months into your pregnancy."

Mellette smiled the smile of a very contented woman as she laid a protective hand on her belly. "Don't I know that."

"So stop looking at that guy over there." Maggie nodded her head, indicating the big hunk of a carpenter working on framing the additional room that would be used as a minor surgery at Eula's House.

"Because you want him?" Mellette teased.

"Please. You know I'm not into relationships."

"Ah, yes. School and work, and more work. An exciting life."

"It is exciting."

"Then why are you looking?"

"I'm not looking so much as…as…admiring the physiology. And I was involved not that long ago."

"Marc the Bland and Raymond the Terrible. You do know how to pick 'em."

Maggie Doucet envisioned Marc for a moment—nice man, no wow factor. When his image disappeared she conjured up Raymond the Terrible—man's body, pig's head.

"Marc was okay, just not…not conversant or interesting. And if you recall, Marc the Bland dumped me. He dumped *me* because I wasn't interesting enough for him."

Maggie and Mellette both laughed, then Mellette continued, "Then entered Raymond the

Rebound, who turned out to be Raymond the Terrible. Misogynist pig of a man."

"I know, I know. You warned me, Mother and Daddy warned me." So had her other five sisters. "I met a street performer down in Jackson Square who was dancing for coins and even he warned me in a mime sort of way."

"Yet you didn't listen to any of us, did you?"

No, she hadn't. Because that's just the way she'd been, looking for absolution and as stubborn as the day was long. Not a good combination. Sure, it was a long, tired story about how she'd been stupid. One known to women the world over. And yes, she'd already admitted it freely. What she'd done hadn't just been stupid. It had been double stupid! Head-in-the-sand time, being dumped by someone she considered bland, then turning to Raymond.

Lesson learned from all that—she wasn't ready to jump back into anything for a long time to come. What she had suited her, kept her as safe as she needed to be. "Not doing it again for a long, long time, if ever."

"Not even with Mr. Tool Belt over there?"

"Especially with Mr. Tool Belt over there. He's…"

"Too tempting?"

"I'm not looking."

"But you took him lemonade yesterday, didn't you? Did you take lemonade to any of the other workers or just him?"

"Just him, but…I did make a pitcher full and left it out there in case any of the others wanted it."

"But he got his from you? Correct?"

"What are you trying to imply?"

"Nothing!"

Maggie snapped, "I just gave the man some lemonade, so don't make a federal case out of it, okay?"

"Which means you *are* interested, being so defensive and all."

"And just where do you get *that?*"

"You also said he's sexy, did you not?"

"I *said* the way he drank his lemonade is sexy. That's not saying he's sexy." Although he was. Very.

"Same thing," Mellette argued.

"No, it's not." Maggie turned and scowled at her sister. "Your pregnancy hormones are acting up again, which is making you irrational."

"How so?"

"You want everybody to be as deliriously happy as you are right now. Even if, like me, they don't want to be. Or if, like me again, they're satisfied with their life the way it is."

"Maybe you want to be happy the way I am, and you just don't know it yet. I was like that when I first met Justin. Wasn't ready to let go of the past and move on. It took me a while to come round, but when I did…"

"You decided the whole world has to act just like you did. Except my world is complicated."

"And mine wasn't?" Mellette asked. "I had to remove a wedding ring given me by someone

I loved very much in order to make room for Justin. And I also had a daughter who was very much involved in my move forward. And you have…" She folded her arms across her fat belly and faked a contemplative frown.

"Let's see. You have none of that. You're moving away from a boring boyfriend, followed by a chauvinist rebound, you're at the top of your law school class, you have a killer job that you claim to love. And that sweaty guy over there keeps looking at you out of the corner of his eye. Nothing about that sounds complicated at all. In fact, it seems pretty straightforward to me."

"I'm in transition. Give me some time."

"Seriously, Maggie? That's the best you can do?"

Maggie took a quick peek at the guy in the jeans, then concentrated on her lemonade. "I'm sure his story is a long, sad one. You know, dumped by the love of his life who ran off to marry a rodeo clown, and now he sits at home alone every night, sniffing the scent of her left on the pillow while petting FruFru, the fluffy white poodle over which they fought for custody."

"First thing is, he's definitely not the poodle type. German shepherd, I think. Yes, he'd definitely have a German shepherd. And, Maggie, if you think he sits home alone every night, you probably don't deserve to serve him lemonade. He's one catchable hunk of man if I've ever seen one, and the only reason he'd be staying home is because he wants to." She took a sip of her lemonade.

"Or he's a serial killer."

"A serial killer with drop-dead-gorgeous blue eyes," Mellette continued.

"They're green," Maggie corrected.

"You looked!"

"And I saw his sandy blond hair, wide shoulders and six-pack abs. Sure, I noticed, and that's not counted as looking. It's being observant. And I'll have a good description ready for the police if he is a serial killer."

"He's a sexy drinker with drop-dead-gorgeous *green* eyes you can describe right down to his abs. So does he have a birthmark?"

"You said they're drop-dead gorgeous," Maggie challenged. "I didn't."

"And you're going to contend they aren't, *madame* lawyer?"

"Not a lawyer yet. And I'm not contending anything other than the fact that they're green." A very nice, tranquil green. "And that he is handsome." With coloring that nearly matched hers, with green eyes just a shade lighter than the green in her eyes.

"Because you were gazing longingly into them."

"If you weren't so pregnant, I'd challenge you to a fight, right here, right now," Maggie said in good-natured fun. "The way we used to when we were kids."

"Remember how Daddy would encourage us, even lay down bets on who'd win the wrestling match? So then we'd go at each other for a while, then Mother would come in and Daddy would pretend he knew nothing about it? Then he'd get all stern and try correcting us, and we'd jump all over him."

Both sisters laughed over the memory.

"Between you and me," Maggie said, "I'm glad you're having a girl. I like the idea that Leonie will have a sister the way I had all of you, and I love the idea of having another niece since the first one I got was so great. I mean, boys are nice, but I don't know how one would fit into the family. We're so used to girls." She was referring to her six other siblings. At age thirty-three, Maggie fell middle in line of the seven Doucet girls. With long, honey-blonde hair and green eyes, she stood out as the different one—she being fair while the others ranged in skin complexion from medium dark to dark.

Being the fairest of the group, people had taken for granted she was also the weakest or most vulnerable. Except that wasn't true. There wasn't a weak, vulnerable Doucet girl in the bunch. Admittedly, Mellette was probably the strongest of them all, and that had helped her through the death of her first husband and into a life with a new love.

Maggie wasn't far behind Mellette in strength, though. Only hers was directed at her career. First a nurse, and now studying to be a lawyer who defended medical malpractice suits—a career change that had come about after her hand, placed directly on a patient's heart with the intent of squeezing the life back into him, had saved him but also caused him an infection.

The ungrateful man hadn't thanked her for saving him but he had sued her for infecting him, which, for a while, had shattered her world and her desire to be in medicine. But like the typical Doucet she was, she'd come back swinging, decided to go to work as a malpractice investigator and, true to her strong nature, decided after that it wasn't enough. Now, with just over nine months to go, she'd be the lawyer fighting back on behalf of the doctors and nurses who got sued unjustly.

"I think Justin's glad it's a girl, too. He loves Leonie, and while he's never said as much, I think he likes the fact that Daddy reigns over an empire of girls. Maybe sees himself in a similar position."

"You want seven, like Mother had?" Maggie questioned.

Mellette shook her head vigorously. "This one, maybe one more. Although I will say that Mr. Drop-Dead-Sexy Carpenter over there looks like he's got some boys in him, in case you want to change the direction of the Doucet family."

"Pregnant or not, I *am* going to wrestle you to the floor," Maggie said, giving her sister a pretend slap on the arm.

"Over what?" Justin Bergeron asked, stepping out onto the front porch. Justin, a general surgeon and part-time general practitioner at Eula's House, was also a medical crime novelist, with a burgeoning screen-writing career added to his résumé.

Both sisters looked up at him and started laughing.

"And I'll take that as my cue to go back inside," Justin said.

"You can stay," Mellette said. "We were just… You know, sister talk." She glanced over at her sister, who was glancing out at the carpenter. "About silly things. You and Amos are welcome to join us out here for lemonade."

Amos Picou, an old Bergeron family friend, stepped past Justin and hurried down the steps. A direct descendent of African lineage, he was a part of the local legend, a friend to all and an all-round good man. "Sorry, ladies, but I'm off to catch me some crawdads for a nice gumbo Justin's going to be fixing later on. Gotta hurry since he's got to get that gumbo on to simmering pretty soon, but later, after I get back, that lemonade will sure hit the spot."

Maggie's eyes opened wider. "Did I hear someone say gumbo? And did I hear an invitation to dinner to help eat some of that gumbo?"

"I'll bet Justin will fix enough for one more, if you want to go over and ask Mr. Tool Belt to join us," Mellette said.

"I'm not going to go ask Mr. Tool Belt anything!" Maggie said, almost too defensively.

Mellette smiled and poured a glass of lemonade. "Just give this to him. Ask him if you want to, or don't." With that, she hurried inside, then watched her sister from the front window.

They were watching him. Probably talking about him. The fact was, he hated lemonade. Had hated it all his life, hated it yesterday when the looker had brought him some, and would hate it just as much this time she brought him a glass. But it was a kind gesture, and he didn't want to seem ungrateful. After all, they'd given him work and, as it turned out, he needed work. He had living expenses to meet and his own house to renovate. Although he was finding it tough working at a medical clinic, being that close to medicine again.

When he'd answered the ad, it had read that this was to be a room addition. He'd assumed a house, as the ad had said to apply at Eula's House. So if he'd known…actually, he'd have probably applied, anyway. But at least he'd have been prepared to spend his days around doctors and nurses. That was the tough part, being around them and not being part of them.

Well, money was money. And lemonade was lemonade. "I appreciate it, ma'am," he said to Maggie, as she handed the glass to him.

"There's more, if you want it," she said. "Up on the front porch. Help yourself. And tell the other workers to help themselves."

"I'll tell the others, but I think one will hit the spot for me, thanks."

"My name's Maggie Doucet, by the way," she said, smiling at him.

"And I'm Alain Lalonde," he replied.

"You're from around here, aren't you? I can tell from the drawl."

"Just moved back from Chicago."

"Chicago? Really? That's where my sister's husband was living when she met him. Justin Bergeron. You've met him, haven't you? He's the doctor on call here.

"Yes, ma'am, I've met him," he said, handing her back the empty glass after downing the lemonade in nearly one gulp, like it was bad medicine. "Now, if you'll excuse me…"

He turned his back and started to walk away. But Maggie called out to him, "Alain, would you care to stay for gumbo tonight? As your drawl indicates you're from around here, I think you'll appreciate a good gumbo for what it is, and my sister's husband is making enough to feed an army."

"Appreciate the invitation, ma'am, but I have other plans." Said politely, because he was grateful for the offer, but he wasn't in a social mood and he didn't want to drag the others down with his attitude. In other words, he knew he'd throw the proverbial wet blanket on the party and he didn't want to do that. "Maybe another time."

"Well, if you change your mind, you're always welcome..."

"Again, thanks. Look, I've got to get back to work, ma'am. The job foreman isn't paying me to stand around and talk. Thanks for the lemonade."

Well, that went badly, Maggie thought as she walked away. Talk about a polite dismissal.

"So?" Mellette asked, even before Maggie was inside the clinic.

"So, what?"

"What did he say?" Mellette asked. "I saw you two talking, so what was it about?"

"He didn't ask me out, if that's what you mean. In fact, I asked him to gumbo tonight and he turned me down."

"Seriously, you asked him to dinner after you told me you wouldn't?"

Maggie shrugged. "I was trying to be friendly. That's all."

"There are six other men on the job site. Did you ask them all, too? Or did you just single out Mr. Tool Belt?"

"His name is Alain Lalonde, and he's the only one I asked. And that's the end of the conversation, as far as I'm concerned because—" she glanced down at the floor "—have you looked at how swollen your ankles are? I want you to go sit down, elevate your legs and leave my love life to me."

"So you're thinking about Alain in terms of your love life?" Mellette teased on her way to her favorite chair.

"I don't want a love life!" Maggie retorted. "Let me repeat myself. I don't want a love life. I have work, I have school, I have my volunteer work here. I have a pregnant sister who needs me to help her. That's enough. *No love life!*"

"Yes, right," Mellette said, as she changed her mind and headed to the stairs, deciding to go to one of the two bedrooms on the second floor for a real rest. "Oh, and Billie Louviere will be here in half an hour for her three-month checkup. Pregnancy's normal, she's doing fine. Justin's available if you need him, but if you don't, tell her hello for me. Oh, and keep an eye on her blood pressure. It hasn't been high but something tells me she might be a candidate for hypertension the further she gets into this pregnancy."

"Her first?"

"After a couple of miscarriages. She's pretty nervous."

"And I'm pretty nervous about your swollen ankles. So go put them up, and call me if you need anything."

"Like lemonade," Mellette teased.

"Leave the lemonade out of this."

Once back outside, Maggie tried not looking for Alain Lalonde, but that was nearly impossible as all the building activity was directly in her line of sight as she sat on the porch. "Okay, so he's good to look at," she said as she poured herself another lemonade. Good to watch, good to turn into a little midday fantasy. After all, there was no harm in looking, was there?

After Billie Louviere's checkup, a couple of walk-ins presented themselves at the clinic, and by midafternoon Maggie had actually seen enough patients that she was getting tired. Not exhausted, but with just the right amount of weariness setting in that she really felt she'd done a good day's work. It was time to go home, though. Eat a quick bowl of gumbo and head on back to town.

Even though she was taking the summer off from school, she still had casework for a couple of legal clients to go over this evening, and she did want to read a chapter in one of her law text-books, if she stayed awake that long.

"Time to get up," she called down the hall to Mellette, who was still napping in Justin's for-mer bedroom. While no one actually lived at Eula's House anymore, named for Justin's grandmother, they kept the upstairs as a residence, hoping that one day it might be turned into a very small hospital ward. The downstairs had been converted into a clinic that maintained a portion of Eula's herbal practice, as well as a proper medical clinic. To outsiders it might seem a confused mishmash of traditions, but to the people of Big Swamp it was where they could seek medical help in whatever form they chose.

"Come on, Mellette. We need to eat, then I've got to get out of here. Go home, go over some case files." She pushed open the bedroom door to look in on her sleeping sister. Then gasped. Her ankles were puffier than before. So were her hands, and even her face, especially around her eyes, looked puffy.

"You okay?" she asked as she approached the bed.

"Headache," Mellette said. "A little nauseous. Think the heat's done me in." She started to sit up, but Maggie gently nudged her back down.

"Stay there. Don't get up yet."

"Why?" Mellette asked. Mellette, a nurse herself, had worked in emergency medicine at New Hope, where their mother, Zenobia, was chief of staff.

"Because you're tired, and tiredness and pregnancy aren't a good combination. I'm going to go downstairs and get you a drink of cold water, so don't get up. Hear me?"

"Hear you," Mellette said, as she dropped back into her pillows and shut her eyes.

Two minutes later Mellette had a blood-pressure cuff strapped to her sister's arm, and two minutes after that she was on her way back downstairs to find Justin.

He was outside, talking to Mr. Tool Belt. "Something's wrong with Mellette," Maggie interrupted, not beating around the bush for a more tactful way to approach it. "I don't do obstetrics so I can't tell for sure, but she's awfully swollen, her blood pressure is on the high end of normal and—"

"Where's she swollen?" Alain Lalonde cut in.

Both Justin and Maggie gave him an inquisitive look. "Feet, ankles, eyelids..." Maggie answered, not sure why she was giving a symptom list to the carpenter.

"Urinary output normal?" Alain went on.

Maggie shrugged, quite surprised by the carpenter's line of questions. "I didn't ask her."

"Nausea, vomiting, headache?" Again from Alain.

"Nausea and headache." More than surprised, she was confused.

"Onset?"

"This afternoon," Maggie said. "Why do you care?"

"Alain was probably the best high-risk obstetrician in Chicago," Justin answered.

"You knew?" Alain asked. "And you didn't ask why I'm here, doing carpentry?"

"A man has a right to his privacy. I didn't want to invade yours."

"So Mellette...I think it may be preeclampsia. If it is, we caught it in time. But I think you'd better be getting your wife to her obstetrician pretty damned fast."

Justin turned to run to the clinic, then paused and signaled for Alain to accompany him, leaving Maggie outside to wonder what had caused a doctor to quit and become a carpenter. Not that there was anything wrong with being a carpenter, because there wasn't. But why had Alain put himself through so many years of medical training just to quit? It made no sense, especially as he was so highly regarded, according to Justin.

So what made a doctor give it up to come to Big Swamp and bang out a clinic expansion? It was a question for which she had no answer. And it was a question for which she was going to find an answer, especially as this man was about to touch her sister. Darned straight, she was going to find an answer.

Instead of going upstairs to Mellette, Maggie went straight to the computer in the office and entered the name Alain Lalonde into a search engine. The first thing that turned up was a head-line about a wounded army doctor who saved the lives of his men and women. They had been under siege and he'd drawn the fire away from his escaping crew and patients. Had been shot in the leg in doing so, spent several weeks in the hospital in rehab. Received a medal.

"Amazing," she said, as the second thing that turned up was of an obstetrician accused in a malpractice suit. Something about performing a Caesarean when it hadn't been necessary. The article said he'd gone against orders from the woman's personal physician and performed an emergency C-section when a normal delivery would have worked.

"And someone sued you for that?" Maggie whispered. It didn't make sense to her as long as the baby had been healthy, which it apparently had been. Was it the lawsuit that had made him quit, or had he just burned out?

"Who are you?" Maggie whispered as she

clicked out of the articles. "Alain Lalonde, just who are you? And why are you working as a carpenter and not an obstetrician?"

CHAPTER TWO

"HOW FAR ALONG are you?" Alain asked as he checked Mellette's blood pressure.

"Twenty-four…no, twenty-five weeks now."

"And when did your symptoms start?" He pumped up the blood-pressure cuff and deflated it slowly.

"A couple of days ago, but only swollen ankles. I honestly didn't think anything about it because of the heat."

"In this heat, swollen ankles are common."

"How high is my blood pressure?"

"One-forty over ninety. Not extremely high, but I wouldn't want to see it going any higher."

Mellette gasped. "And the baby?"

"I don't have anything here to do any tests, but I heard the heartbeat, and it was strong."

Justin and Maggie, who'd finally joined them, sighed in relief.

"Look, you need to be in the hospital at least for the night so your doctor can get tests done. I think you have a mild case of preeclampsia, which can be controlled by drugs and lots of rest, but we need a blood panel, and most of all we need to get a fetal monitor on you. The problem is, the trip out of here is rougher than I want you to take." He looked up at Maggie. "Is there any way to get a helicopter in here?"

"No!" Mellette gasped.

"It's for your own good, Mellette," Alain said. "But most of all it's for the baby's safety."

Mellette shut her eyes and a tear squeezed out the side and trickled down her cheek. Immediately, Justin was at her side, pulling her into his arms. "Alain's a good doctor," he said. "If he thinks we need to evacuate you by air, that's what we'll do."

Even before Mellette had a chance to agree, Maggie was on the phone, making the arrangements. "Thirty minutes?" she questioned. "We'll get her down to the pickup spot as fast as we can."

"Already?" Alain asked, clearly impressed.

"Done deal. We need to get her down to the grocery in Grandmaison where an ambulance will take her out to Flander's Meadow where she'll be picked up. The ambulance will be there in half an hour, so I'd suggest we get going. If that's okay with you?" she asked Alain.

"Perfect plan." He gave her an admiring glance as she helped Justin bundle up his wife for the trip.

"Please," Mellette said, "I can walk down the stairs."

"And I can carry you down just as easily," Justin said.

"I want you to come along, as well," Alain said to Maggie. "I don't anticipate anything happening, but I want you to keep watch on her blood pressure while I drive."

"I can do that."

"It's going to be that proverbial bumpy ride."

Maybe it was, but Maggie was glad with everything inside her that Alain was there taking charge. No matter what the article said, she trusted him.

Maggie stared up into the sky as the helicopter lifted off, carrying Justin and Mellette. She'd already called her parents, who would be at the other end when it landed. And she'd called her sisters, as well as Pierre Chaisson, Mellette's brother-in-law from her first marriage, who would watch Leonie when everybody else was at the hospital. "You never think in terms of a pregnancy having difficulties when the mother is in such good shape. I mean, prenatal problems are for other people."

"They're for everybody, Maggie. Sometimes they can be predicted, sometimes they can't, sorry to say. I mean, Mellette doesn't seem to carry any of the risk factors, but you see the results on someone who's perfectly fine. It's frustrating for everybody."

"But Mellette's going to be okay, isn't she?"

"Once they get her blood pressure stabilized she'll be much better. The thing is, she's really going to have to be careful now, because she's not far enough along to deliver. But we have our ways of taking care of these problems, lots of new drugs and techniques, and odds are your sister is going to do just fine and deliver a healthy baby at the end of her pregnancy."

"Wish you could make guarantees," Maggie said on a sigh, as Alain slipped an arm around her shoulder. "Or promises."

"Wish I could, too. But the one thing I can guarantee is that you did a good job, catching it quickly and responding the way you needed to. A lot of women think all that pregnancy puffiness is just part of the course. Mellette got lucky."

"That's what nurses are supposed to do."

"You're a nurse? I guess I'm not surprised because of the way you responded, but I didn't know that. I'd heard you were in law school."

"I am, but I'm a nurse first."

"Busy lady. But a very astute one. Your training shows."

"Thank you," she said. "I come from a long line of medical people. I think it comes naturally when your name is Doucet."

"Doucet, as in...?"

She nodded, enjoying the feel of his strong arm. It was steady, something to give her comfort. "Yes, *that* Doucet family. Fortunately, or unfortunately, we're known far and wide. Or should I say my parents are." She smiled. "The rest of us just try to maintain the family reputation as best we can."

Alain chuckled. "Well, you maintained it today. Did it proud. So I wonder if that gumbo is still simmering, because I could sure go for a bowl of it right about now."

"I'll bet it is," Maggie said halfheartedly.

"You want to go to the hospital, don't you?"

She nodded.

"Then here's the plan. Gumbo first, and that will give the doctors enough time to get your sister looked at and under treatment. Besides, she's not going to be allowed any visitors for a while—just her husband, and I'm sure your mother. So you might as well wait a little while here with me, then I'll drive you in to the hospital."

"You'd do that?"

"It's not out of the way. My…house is just a few blocks from New Hope, which is where I'm assuming she'll be going, so it's no big deal."

"Then I say let's go have some gumbo."

"So here's the thing," Maggie said to Alain over gumbo. "I've been giving this some thought. We need a doctor here. I'm here part time, and my sisters manage to squeeze in some hours, along with my dad when we need him. Mellette and Justin are the driving force, though, and that's over with for a while now. So I need someone who, first, is licensed here, which you are, according to the internet, and also who can guarantee me something near full-time hours for a little while, as Justin's going to be staying home more to watch over Mellette. With both of them gone, that leaves the clinic closed a good bit of the time, and since you're not working as a doctor right now..."

"I'm not working as a doctor, period. Hence the hammer in my hand." She'd been reading about his past and he wasn't sure if he liked that or not. It was all still so...touchy with him.

"But I read up on you. You're an obstetrician and a war hero. You ran a military hospital in Afghanistan so I'm sure you're up to some work here, in this clinic."

"Ran a hospital, past tense. And if you read up on me, you'll know why."

"You were involved in a lawsuit and I'm sorry about that. Sincerely sorry it happened to you. But if every doctor who got sued stepped away from medicine, there wouldn't be any doctors left."

He cringed. "It wasn't that simple. But that's the bottom line, yes. I did get sued, and the hospital stepped back from me because the people suing me are, shall we say, prominent. They make big donations to the hospital. I did what I believed was right, which left a perfect bikini body with a scar, and the hospital walked away from me. Took a step back, threw collective hands into the air and told me I was on my own."

"Which is enough to make you bitter, and I understand that. And like I said, I'm sorry about that," Maggie said in earnestness. "It's never easy, getting sued. I saw how it devastated my parents the few times they were sued. But they were lucky that the hospital stood behind them and they came out victorious. I take it you're not doing so well in your lawsuit?"

"To say the least," he repeated. "And it's not just the lawsuit itself. It's all the other things on the periphery that get to you."

"What do you mean?"

"You can't get it off your mind. You go over everything you did, wondering if you missed something or left out something that was crucial. You wonder what you could have done differently that might have changed the outcome. But, damn, in the end it was just a scar. She has a perfect baby boy to show for it."

"Well, your insurance company should figure it out. They don't pay out on bad or false claims."

"That's the other part. I took two years off and went to serve in the military before the lawsuit was filed and the hospital revoked my insurance in that time and fired me while I was laid up in rehab, trying to figure out whether or not I'd ever walk again. So I'm hanging out there on my own in this. Welcome home, Captain Lalonde."

Maggie's eyes widened. "I did read about your injury, and I'm sorry."

"Old news," he said. "I recovered. But while I was focused on that, the hospital did me in. And the thing is…"

"There's no loyalty," Maggie said. "It was owed you, and they took it away. But after that long?"

"Statute of limitations in Illinois is generous. The thing is, I talked to the woman who's suing me—"

"Your attorney let you do that?" Maggie interrupted.

"I don't have an attorney. Can't afford one."

"And the hospital where you worked really, truly isn't backing you up at all?"

"They claim my insurance coverage ended when I went into the military and became a military doctor, therefore they're under no obligation to cover me in a suit that was filed after I left the military. I mean, there was almost a three-year lapse in there."

"Seriously?" Maggie said indignantly. "That's what they're trying to pull?"

He shrugged. "I got some pro bono advice, which was basically to try to reach a settlement. But the settlement they want is higher than I can afford. I damaged a model's perfect body with a scar and they want a bite out of me."

"But the baby was healthy."

"It was in fetal distress. Her own doctor wasn't responding to the calls. They came in, I got assigned and knew there was no way she was going to push that baby out in time, maybe not at all because her pelvis was so small, so I did what I had to do. And now, with the lawsuit hanging over my head, no one back in Chicago will hire me because along with the lawsuit they went after my reputation, so here I am working as a carpenter, probably not inclined to ever go back into medicine, anyway. Bottom line is I appreciate the offer you gave me, but I come with built-in liabilities."

"Maybe you do, but are you contented to stay a carpenter? After all your years of education and experience, are you ready to simply throw in the towel and keep that hammer handy?"

"I've had a couple of friends who were knocked to their knees by malpractice suits. It was ugly.

And while the insurance usually pays up one way or another, there's no way to fix a damaged reputation. For me, that's as important as anything in this whole mess."

"And it's a stigma for life, if you don't have the right people representing you. My parents have both been unjustly sued—my mother on behalf of the hospital more times than I can count, and it's always a horrible time for her. For Daddy, too, when he got sued, because of all the emotions involved."

"Then you understand."

"More than know, Alain. That's what I do."

"What do you mean?"

"I'm a registered nurse, and I work part time in medicine just to keep up, also because I love patient care. But I'm also a medical malpractice investigator, and within a few months I'll be an attorney who's going to specialize in med malpractice cases, not representing the people doing the suing but the medical personnel being sued. Besides putting on a vigorous defense where it's deserved, I also want to do some reputation fixing. The thing is, insurance companies are so eager to simply give in and settle, but that doesn't vindicate the doctor or nurse being sued who doesn't deserve it. Like you, for example. You'd never seen this patient before, and she presents with fetal distress. Yet she's wanting to get into your pockets for something that wasn't your fault."

"It's not about the money. They have enough for two lifetimes. It's all ego. I suppose they want a story to tell. And they sure as hell got it. On top of that, he wants to run for some elected office and campaign on medical reform as part of his platform. He just happens to want to build that platform on my back."

Maggie paused for a moment, then a smile slowly spread to her face. "Then here's what I propose. I'll have to check with my superiors first, because I'm just the investigator. But if I can convince them to take you on as a client, in return I'd like hours here at the clinic. We'll pay you, of course. Not much, but some kind of stipend for living expenses."

"You can work in Illinois?"

"We have a registered agent in Illinois so yes, I can work there. And the thing is, Alain, while this isn't the kind of action that's going to put money in your pocket, unless you want to countersue, which I wouldn't recommend since you turning around and suing back turns you into some kind of aggressor you don't want to become, it's one that will prevent you from having to go through this alone. And there's a good possibility we can restore your reputation once we win it and it's over with.

"In other words, the best outcome would be giving you some peace of mind, and maybe the will to go back out there and practice medicine on a full-time basis. So…interested?" Her heart really did go out to the man. He was taking a beating he didn't deserve. Even without all the facts, it sounded as if he'd unwittingly stepped in then gotten hammered with a situation that couldn't have possibly been salvaged.

"Maybe," he said cautiously. "The thing is, if they sue me they can't really get anything. I wasn't kidding when I said I needed this job as a carpenter to get by. So wouldn't it be just as easy to let them sue then find out I'm not worth two nickels? I mean, I'm living in my aunt's house, fixing it up for her. She's moved to Florida and told me I can do with it what I want. She'll deed it over to me in due course if I want the place, but I don't want it right now because if I'm being sued I don't want them taking her house."

"Your reputation's worth more than a couple of nickels, isn't it?"

"It used to be."

"You've got a mighty good reputation in the military. Got a medal of honor, didn't you?"

"Are you just full of facts about me?"

"Just read the headlines, not the details." She smiled. "And that headline needs to be protected, Alain. You did something good, and you deserve to be proud about it rather than simply giving in to defeat."

"I'm not defeated. More like practical."

"Which is why I want to practice medical defense law. Someone's coming at you, going to ruin you if they can, and you don't deserve it."

"So what if you do get your law firm to take me on? What happens?"

"First, they'll assign me to investigate the case. And if I do say so myself, I'm the best at what I do."

He chuckled. "And modest, too."

"Only when I have to be."

"Anybody ever called you a pit bull?" he asked.

"A time or two. The thing is, I believe in what I do. Doctors and nurses are an easy target, especially doctors who are required to carry so much insurance. My mother runs a hospital where doctors are sued unjustly all the time, and it takes so much away from the patient care she should be giving because she has to get involved in the legal proceedings.

"The worst, though, was my dad. He suffered a huge suit, and it depressed him for weeks. He didn't do anything wrong, and the hospital eventually just settled on his behalf. He wanted to defend himself, though, and he never felt good that by settling it seemed like he was guilty of medical negligence. It broke his heart, and that hurt all of us."

"Which is when you decided you wanted to be a crusader?"

"Not a crusader. Just someone who wanted to make sure that the innocent weren't being punished. And I'm not saying that all cases are unfair, because I've seen some that are well deserved. But I've seen too many that are not."

Alain took a sip of his water then squinted up at the sun. "So what you would want in return are hours at the clinic, doing what I'm assuming will be general medicine."

"Are you good with herbal medicine? Because we do a bit of that, as well."

"I've never gone near the stuff."

"Then that's where I can help, because Mellette's been teaching me."

"You're going to be my nurse?"

"Probably. But I do have my other work, as well as law school."

"Meaning you never sleep."

"Meaning I sleep only when I have to."

"Well, I do have a commitment to work on the addition, and Tom Chaisson—"

"Mellette's other brother-in-law from her first marriage," Maggie interrupted.

"You keep things very cozy down here, don't you?"

"We try to," she said.

"Anyway, Tom just made me project foreman. He's got another job in Baton Rouge that he's got to oversee, so he asked me to take on this project for him. And I can't back out on that. So if I agree to this, when I don't have a stethoscope around my neck I'll be wearing tools on my hips. Can you deal with that?"

Could she deal with that? The fact that she

could still watch him in carpenter mode was an added bonus. "I can," she said, her voice just a bit on the wobbly side.

"Then I guess we have a deal. You take my case to your law firm and see what they have to say about it, and I'll work here as your doctor on call."

"You can live here, too, if you want," she added. "Upstairs, in one of the bedrooms."

"Might not be a bad idea, as I've got my aunt's house practically gutted and I'm reduced to living on a cot and cooking on a hot plate. Her house was one of those projects that the more I got into it, the more I found that needed fixing." He grinned. "And it's a big old plantation house, turning into a big old plantation money pit."

"Well, no promises or anything, but I do have some pull at New Hope, which could be a consideration for you after we get your lawsuit straightened out."

"Anyway, I think it's time to get you on the road. I expect that by the time we get there the doctors will know more about what's going on with your sister."

Maggie reached over and gave his hand a squeeze. "You're a good man, Dr. Lalonde, and it's my intention to make sure you hang on to that reputation."

"I like your passion," he said.

And she liked his abs.

"So you're a doctor?" Mellette said. She was on bed rest now but allowed to travel out to Eula's House with Justin when he took calls there. Her condition had much improved in a couple of days and for now she was allowed light activity.

"Depends on the time of day," Alain said as he eyed her ankles.

"They're much better, Doctor. Swelling's gone down, and they're almost back to normal. You caught it in the early stages and my physician is treating me for preeclampsia. He doesn't think I'm going to have any strong complications, though. And while I have to curtail my activities, I'm not on total bed rest yet."

"As long as you're sensible," Alain warned.

"That's what everybody keeps telling me. And with six sisters, trust me, I'm never alone to do something insensible, not that I would. But I just wanted to thank you for helping me, and for taking over the clinic."

"Your doctor's aware you're coming out to Big Swamp?"

"He's aware, and he's consented, provided I strictly limit my activities to giving advice from a lounging position. Got to have someone to oversee the medicinals," she said, smiling. "Maggie's coming along in her knowledge of herbs, though. I expect she'll know everything she needs to in the next couple of weeks. She's awfully smart."

"Nurse, herbal practitioner and lawyer-to-be. I'd call that well-rounded."

"Somebody talking about me?" Maggie asked,

as she took a seat next to her sister on the porch swing.

"Saying horrible things," Mellette teased.

Alain liked the way they interacted. He'd never had brothers and sisters. In fact, his parents had been very old when he'd been born—one of those menopausal miracles that happened to a couple who'd been barren for twenty-five years and had adjusted their lives accordingly.

While he loved his folks dearly, there'd never been any youth in his life. With a mother who had been near fifty when he was born, and a dad in his mid-fifties, he'd been raised in an older world than most of his friends, and as a consequence he'd always seemed too old and stodgy. There'd been no youthful pranks, not even when he'd been in college. No frat parties. No wild and crazy dates. Just seriousness, studying and responsibility.

Yet when he saw the way Maggie interacted with her sister, it caused him to realize what he'd missed out on. And made him feel a little envious. Stirred something up in him. "She told me what a bad girl you were when you were young."

"Maybe just a little bit. But I wasn't in it alone. There was always another sister joining in, then blaming it all on me."

"Who, me?" Mellette asked, laughing and holding her belly to stop it from jiggling.

"You, Sabine, Delphine, Ghislaine, Lisette or Acadia."

Alain shook his head. "It's hard to imagine your mother having seven of you and still running one of the best medical centers in the South."

"We're strong women," Maggie said. "Had parents to support that in us."

"Strong, as in overachievers?" he asked.

"Call it what you want," Maggie went on. "But that's who we are. My mother was raised in an era where women were just on the brink of coming into their own, only in her family, because they were of a certain social status..."

"And from a very traditional Southern family," Mellette added.

"That, too," Maggie agreed. "Anyway, what was expected from her was to be just like her mother, who was…I guess the best way to describe our grandmother is a social butterfly. That's the way she was raised, and it was the world in which she raised our mother. For my grandmother, who is involved in more charitable work than anyone I've ever seen, it works. Her life exists for her causes, and she works hard at them, but she also finds time to sit down to tea with various friends every day of the week.

"But for my mother…that social hour of tea was wasted when there were things to do. She was hard-driven, I guess you could call her. So instead of following in the family tradition, she started one of her own. And we all seem to be following her example in one way or another." She smiled, then added, "As overachievers."

"So what about your family, Alain?"

"Teachers. My mother taught high school math

and my father taught college chemistry. They're both retired now, living in a condo on a Costa Rican beach."

"No brothers or sisters?" Maggie asked.

"Just me. A late-in-life kid who surprised the hell out of my parents when I popped into their lives."

"Sounds like an interesting story," Mellette said.

"More like typical. We were just an ordinary family. No prestige. No bells and whistles."

"But close?" Maggie asked.

"More so now than when I was younger. But I've grown up. It happens to most of us sooner or later."

"And what do they think about you not practicing medicine any longer?" Maggie asked.

"Actually, they don't know I've given up the stethoscope for a hammer. They think I'm in Louisiana practicing medicine, and as far as I'm concerned, that's the way I want to leave it."

Maggie gave him a questioning look. "Because they're older?"

"Because they made a lot of sacrifices for me when I went to medical school, and I sure as hell don't want them knowing they wasted their money."

"It wasn't wasted," Mellette said, as Justin stepped out on the porch. "Look what you did for me. That, in and of itself, says a lot about your ability. Now all you need to do is let my sister get to work on your case and get you back where you belong on a full-time basis, rather than squeezing it in while you're letting your drywall spackle dry."

"My wife's opinionated," Justin said, taking Mellette by the arm and leading her down the stairs. "And on that note I'm going to wish you both a good afternoon and escort her home. The waiting room is cleared, and barring any emergencies or walk-ins, you're free for the rest of the day. Although I wouldn't count on it, because I heard that Ivy Comfort may be having a bout of rheumatism." He smiled. "As they say, heard it through the grapevine, which is alive and well in these parts."

Alain's expression turned to panic. "I don't treat rheumatism."

"But I do," Maggie said. "And it's me she'll want to be seeing for some special tea and maybe a liniment we make that's—"

Alain held up his hand to stop her. "I'm going to trust that you know what you're doing, and leave it at that. If Miss Comfort would like any medical treatment, I'll be glad to see what I can do. Maybe prescribe a mild anti-inflammatory drug or—"

"She won't take your prescription," Maggie warned as Justin and Mellette walked away. "It's been a real challenge here to prescribe traditional medicine. Most of the people are willing to tolerate it, since it's all they can get without leaving the area. But we have a few hold-outs who absolutely refuse to give in to modern ways, and Ivy Comfort just happens to be one of them. So Eula gave her some herbs that seemed to help, then Mellette took over after Eula died, and now that end of the practice is being passed along to me. Along with any regular nursing duties that come up."

"Your family's gotten so involved here. I wouldn't have thought that, given your mother's status, you'd have been inclined to."

Maggie shrugged. "Initially, it was because my sister came to help out Justin's grandmother, who was an herbal practitioner. The people here trusted her for over half a century, and when she died the position of herbal practitioner sort of fell to Mellette because the people here trusted her, too. They didn't trust Justin, who wanted to practice nothing but traditional medicine, and a lot of them still haven't come round to his way of thinking. But I suppose because Eula trusted Mellette, and I'm her sister, that's why they trust me."

"Then what's that say about me? I'm just an

interloping medical doctor who's not going to put forth any kind of effort to prescribe herbs."

"What it says is that you'll have a tough time. There will be some who accept you unconditionally because you're a doctor, and some who'll accept you marginally because they trust Mellette, Justin and me. Then there will be those, like Ivy Comfort, who won't even acknowledge you." She smiled. "Ever."

"Even if I prescribe an anti-inflammatory for her that does more for her than her herbs?"

"Even if you prescribe an anti-inflammatory for her that cures her rheumatism. That's just the way she is. The way a lot of people here are, and you'll have to accept it. As in not taking it personally when Ivy walks in that door and instructs you to fix her a cup of coffee."

Alain laughed. "Actually, I make a pretty mean cup of coffee, so Miss Ivy and I might just hit it off."

"Don't count on it," Maggie warned, smiling. She liked this man. Liked his seriousness, liked the way he fixed on his task. And, Lord knew, she'd watched a good bit of that these past few days.

"So what you're telling me is that in order to get along in these parts, I'd be better off sticking to my carpentry work?"

"Probably."

He smiled, and arched wicked, sexy eyebrows. "Then I guess that's what I'd better get back to. If you need me…" He raised fingers to his mouth and faked a whistle.

"Trust me, I will." With a fair amount of pleasure, actually. "Oh, and, Alain, I'll know more from my law firm tomorrow on whether or not they're going to take on your case. The partners are going to have a meeting on it first thing in the morning."

"Any indication, one way or another?"

She shook her head. "Although I can say that they usually go with my recommendations. In fact, the only thing they ever fully reject is my suggestion for the office Christmas party. I like glitz and glitter and all the trimmings, and they like to keep it...sedate."

"You don't like sedate?"

"For a holiday, it's boring. And why be boring when you can be over-the-top?"

"An over-the-top overachiever." He gave her a slight bow as he stepped off the front porch. "I bow to your abilities."

"And I accept that bow," she said, laughing. Yes, she really liked this man. Now all she had to do was get him out of the mess he was in. Which meant, if the partners took him on as a client, no mixing of business and pleasure. Too bad, as she had an idea the pleasure part could have been way over-the-top, as well.

CHAPTER THREE

SHE HELD OUT her hand for him to see a grouping of the tiniest marks. They *hurted* her, she told him. "My ouchie." In reality the wound was from the common stinging nettle, a very uncomfortable plant with which to make contact. But it was nothing that required medical attention, which made Alain wonder why she was here.

"And you came to me all by yourself?" he asked, quite touched by the girl. Her big brown eyes were sad, and huge fat tears welled up in them.

"'Cause you're the doctor. Aunt Gertrude told me to come over here, that you could fix it for me."

He was flattered and angry at the same time. Lilly, as she called herself, couldn't have been more than six, maybe not even that old, and a child that age had no business wandering around the bayou all by herself. "Well, your Aunt Gertrude was right about that. I can." A nice stream of hot water usually did the trick, or a generous coating of calamine lotion.

"Dandelion works," Maggie offered as she entered the exam room, carrying a glass of juice for the child.

Alain shook his head. "Nothing herbal…"

"Just saying," she quipped as she handed Lilly the apple juice.

He nodded as he led Lilly over to the sink and held her hand under the water while she was distracted, drinking her juice. "So no one's with her?" he asked, trying to sound matter-of-fact.

"Not a soul. Miss Lilly Anna Montrose was a big girl today and came all the way here from Grandmaison by herself."

Grandmaison, a good two-mile walk. Now he was downright mad, angry enough to spit nails at someone. "Well, then, I'd say Miss Lilly was one brave little girl today. That was a mighty long walk for her to take all by herself."

"People around here are independent," Maggie said, but not in defense of Lilly's aunt, who'd sent her off alone. "They start that independence young in some cases."

"Too young," he said, looking at the hand where the nettles had stung the child.

"Can't say that I disagree. I was as surprised as you when she showed up here a little while ago. Oh, and she also brought payment." Maggie held it up. It was a quarter.

"Is that your money?" Alain asked the girl.

She nodded. "I've been saving up. Aunt Gertrude told me I had to use it to pay for my 'pointment. Is it enough? 'Cause I have two more at home."

"As it turns out, that's exactly what I charge for fixing a nettle sting."

She handed the empty glass back to Maggie. "Thank you," she said. "That was very good."

"Would you like some more?" Maggie asked.

The little girl nodded shyly. "All we ever get to drink is water. Sometimes tea, if we can afford it."

"Look, Lilly, I need to go get some special medicine to put on your hand. Would you mind sitting up on the table until I come back?"

"Okay," she said, then smiled. "It doesn't hurt so much now. Maybe it was the apple juice."

"Then I think we should give you some apple juice to take home with you, in case it starts hurting later on. Do we have enough to send some with Miss Lilly?" he asked Maggie.

"Full supply of it, Doctor," she said, stepping back as Alain lifted the child up onto the exam table.

"We'll be right back," he said to Lilly, then followed Maggie into the hall. "She's malnourished, unkempt, I doubt she's ever seen a dentist or a doctor and God only knows what kind of parasites or other bugs she's infested with. And a two-mile walk?"

"I need to figure out what to do about her,"

Maggie said. "Because if her aunt's house is like what I'm expecting..."

"Then we can't put that child back in there. Do you know her aunt, by any chance?"

Maggie shook her head. "But I know a child social services worker and I think I'll give her a call before we decide what we need to do about Lilly."

"What I need to do is not send her back into a home where an adult would allow her to come here by herself."

"Don't jump the gun, Alain. We haven't even seen that house, and we sure don't know the circumstances..."

"Yeah, well, I can only guess!" he snapped. "I saw those conditions in Afghanistan, where children were robbed of their youth, like Lilly is. So much poverty, so many health problems..." His eyes went distant for a moment. "Landmine victims...just children. You can't even begin to imagine..."

Maggie laid a comforting hand on his arm.

"No, I can't," she said softly. "And I'm sorry you had to see such atrocities."

"Seeing them is one thing, but living them is another." Said in bitter despair. "And not being able to do anything to fix it."

"I can't say that I even have a clue what you're talking about. My life, for the most part, has been pretty sheltered. Never any hardships, never any threats."

"Then you were lucky. Because a lot of the world out there is ugly. Like I think Lilly's world is probably ugly, too. Look, she needs a bath, Maggie. And a good head scrubbing as I'm pretty sure she's got lice. Could you do that for me and give her a good going over to see what else we can find?"

"And clean clothes," Maggie said, knowing there were no little-girl clothes at Eula's House. "I'll call my dad and see if he can bring something out for her. Shoes, too. I'm betting there are still some things left over from one of our childhoods stashed away in the attic."

"He'd do that?"

"My dad is a real softie when it comes to little girls. He always threatened to trade a few of us in on boys, but I think he liked sitting at the head of an all-female kingdom, being adored by his flock."

She truly liked Alain's sympathies. More than that, she was surprised how easily they were jostled to the surface. He seemed more like a man who held everything in, yet the instant Lilly had walked into the clinic and held out her tiny, grimy hand, he'd melted. And not just a little. "I have money," she'd proclaimed. But she'd had more than that. In that very instant she'd had Alain's heart. And a very tender heart it was indeed.

"So what's the prognosis?" Alain asked an hour later.

"Lice, like you thought. I did the treatment, and cut her hair a little to get rid of some of the mats. And she's about ten pounds under her ideal weight, a little on the small side for a child her age. She has very bad skin, lots of bruises and cuts. Missing some baby teeth. No education, no attempt to teach her to read. But she's very bright. And she loved her bath. I found an old bottle of bubble bath left over from Eula, and I think this child would have stayed in the water and played all day long if we'd let her."

"Any health concerns?"

"Nothing significant that I could find. Heart and lungs sounded good, eyes are clear, ears turned out fine after I cleaned them. She does have a few open sores, probably infected bug bites. No real signs of physical abuse. More like extreme neglect. All in all, I think she's a healthy child, but I would like her to be seen by a pediatrician at some point for a complete exam."

He sighed heavily. "So what do we do in the meantime?"

"I've talked to my friend from Child Services and she's going to come investigate, but that may take a couple of days. If we think the child is in imminent danger we can surrender her to the authorities and they'll put her into the children's home until the case can be investigated."

"Which isn't a solution, either."

Maggie shrugged. "You could keep her here, if you get her aunt's consent. Provided her aunt is her legal guardian."

"And just what would I do with a child?"

"Protect her. Look, this is a gray area in the law, because the authorities don't like to separate a child from his or her family without just cause, and so far we don't know if we have that cause. We suspect it, but suspicion isn't enough."

"Bet we'll find some pretty damning evidence it if we go over to Grandmaison and knock on her aunt's door." Alain clicked into his cell phone and dialed a number. "You up to babysitting for an hour?" he said as Maggie brought a freshly scrubbed Lilly into the kitchen. She was wearing a shirt that came down to her ankles. It was cinched around the waist with some gauze strips. And she was barefoot. Clean, though. Clean and beautiful, with bright eyes and a shy smile. "I have a house call to make and I seem to have found myself a little friend to watch over for the time being."

Amos Picou, on the other end of the phone, was more than happy to do the honors, and he was there within ten minutes, immediately engaging Lilly in stories of Big Swamp. "He comes around every day, checking the work we're doing, making sure we're doing it up to Eula's standards. He seems like a nice man," Alain explained.

"A very nice man," Maggie said, changing out of her work shoes into ankle-high walking boots.

"We're driving," Alain told her.

"Maybe that's your intention, but once we get to Grandmaison, there's no telling what we'll be doing or where we'll be going." She tied her long hair up in a bandanna and, as was her habit, she grabbed up her backpack full of medical supplies. Looking more like an outdoor adventurer than a nurse, in cargo shorts and a T-shirt, Maggie was the first out the door and likewise the first one to her car.

"You're driving?" Alain asked, running to keep up with her. Like Maggie, he had hiking boots, only they were laced together and slung over his shoulder.

"My car, and I know the roads. Seems like I'm the logical one."

"Not complaining," Alain said as he hopped in alongside her. In a split second they were off, speeding down the road as Amos sat on the front porch, entertaining Lilly.

"Are you always going to get this involved?" Maggie asked, once they were underway. "Because there are a lot of people out here who could use some help. That's why I keep coming back. Mellette asked me out here the first time and it became addictive, giving medical care on the most fundamental of all levels."

"I'm not involved," he said. "Just concerned."

"Lie to yourself, Alain. Lie as much as you want, but to the people looking in, you're involved. Don't know why, not going to ask questions, not going to pry. But let me warn you. When you get too involved, it breaks your heart."

"Has your heart been broken?" he asked.

"Be more specific. Has my heart been broken by…a man, by medicine, by life in general?"

"Any, or all."

"Yes to all, I suppose. I've had a couple of relationships that totally fizzled because…because I am who I am. One man just bored me and the other insulted me. And both of them thought I should change into the woman they wanted me to be. One dumped me, I dumped the other. Good riddance to both."

"So you're an overachiever and a hard case. What other attributes are you hiding, Maggie?"

She smiled. "The ones where I march to my own drummer, as they say. Learned it from my mother, polished it thanks to Mellette, who takes stubbornness to an art form. And tempered it thanks to my kind-hearted, sweet father." She swerved to avoid a bump in the road, and in doing so hit another bump in the road. "Damn it," she muttered.

"A little temper, too?" he asked.

"No. A lot of temper. Most of it reined in most of the time."

"Remind me to stay on your good side," he teased.

"Trust me, there are days when I don't have a good one."

"Which is why you want to become a lawyer?"

She laughed. "Nothing quite so complex. I'm going to be a lawyer because I like to argue with people I perceive to be in the wrong. Oh, and win. I love winning."

"Winning for yourself, not for your client."

"One and the same. When I'm involved, it's all the way. Kind of like you and children you see as neglected or abused. When you're involved, it's all the way."

"Is my heart hanging out on my sleeve that much?" he asked.

"It is, but it's a good look." A very good look.

She liked a big hunk of a man who also had a gentle side. It gave him nice balance, which, in turn, balanced her quite well, too. That was, if they got involved enough for her to even stay balanced. Which wasn't going to happen since she wasn't at the right place in her life to take on any more than she already had. Call it bad timing or misaligned karma, or whatever you liked. Alain Lalonde was one of the good ones who was simply going to have to slip on by.

The journey came to an end at a contraption that looked like an old house trailer with several shanty add-ons. Chicken bones and plastic milk cartons littered the ground outside the structure, along with various other indescribable bits of refuse. Judging from the looks of things, the inhabitants here simply opened up their windows and tossed out their trash. The newer the trash, the more flies buzzing around it.

"It's worse than I thought," Maggie said, following behind Alain up an intentional clearing that served as a path leading from where several rusted pickup trucks were parked, past a grave-yard for refrigerators, stoves and other cast-aside appliances, right past an old claw-foot bathtub filled with dirt and berry bushes, and on up to the door, where a welcome mat sat askew on a rotting wooden step-up. "How could anybody raise a child in this squalor?"

"Not very well," Alain said.

She appreciated the safety behind him. He was so large, with such broad shoulders, she felt for-tified by his brute strength. And while she didn't know if this was a situation that required protec-tion, having it there in the form of a very buff man sure didn't hurt. "So what's the plan once we knock on the front door?" she whispered nervously.

"Hope someone answers."

"Someone rational," she added. "Because from the look of this place, that could be a tall order."

"Hope you're wrong about that, because I in-tend on telling them they're not getting Lilly back and asking them to sign the consent form you drew up." One that allowed him to keep Lilly for an unspecified amount of time until her future welfare could be determined.

"Have you given any thought as to what happens if they refuse to sign?"

"I could just keep her, as they sent her to me. Or if worse comes to worst, surrender her to the authorities. However it works out, she's not coming back here, into this mess." Alain raised his hand to knock on the front door, but in midrise the door swung back to reveal a woman who could have been Lilly forty years into the future. "Good afternoon," he greeted the filthy woman standing in front of him. She was rail thin, with frowsy hair, and looked like she hadn't seen the good side of a washcloth in weeks.

She said nothing.

"I'm, um...I'm Dr. Lalonde...the one Lilly came to see this afternoon."

"She got in the sticker bushes even after I told her to be careful, stupid girl. I was hoping you could put some sense in that head of hers." The woman looked beyond him. "Where is she? She's got chores to do and supper to help get on the table in a little while."

In the background, Alain could distinguish the form of a large man in a white T-shirt and camouflage overalls, and he wondered if poor Lilly had been raised to wait on this couple. He could almost picture it, and it made him cringe. "She's safe, Mrs. Montrose."

"Name's Aucoin. Gertrude Aucoin."

"Mrs. Aucoin," he corrected. "And she's not coming back here. I was concerned about her overall condition, and I've called the authorities, who will be stepping in on Lilly's behalf."

For a moment Gertrude Aucoin almost looked relieved. Then her face contorted into anger. "You got no rights. You hear me? You got no right to keep the girl."

"Why did you send her to me with a case of stinging nettle?" he asked.

"Don't know what you're talking about. That

child was howling something awful, after getting stuck up the way she was, and I just did the responsible thing, sending her off to get it treated."

Maggie saw that look of relief again. It was there in the woman's eyes, and unmistakable. Something maybe only another woman might recognize. "We'll take good care of her," she said so quietly she almost whispered the words. "But we can't let her come back here, into this. And we need to have you sign a paper that lets us take care of Lilly until we can figure out what's best for her."

Alain held out the paper, along with a pen.

"He won't be happy about this," Gertrude said. "That child has chores that need doing and Joe's not going to be happy at all."

"And that child shows sign of neglect," Alain said, trying to stay calm on the outside when nothing inside him was.

Gertrude looked up, and he saw it in her eyes again. "Do you need help, as well?" he asked.

She shook her head. "He wouldn't dare touch me, or else who would take care of him? But I'm afraid for the child—he hasn't hit her yet, but the way he's been looking at her with such meanness in his eyes, I'm afraid he will…" She took a quick glance over her shoulder to make sure *he* wasn't standing behind her. "Joe never wanted her here, but we didn't have a choice. They just dropped her off one day after my sister died, and told me there was no one else to take care of her."

"You understand why we can't let her come back, don't you?"

The woman nodded as she took the pen. "I don't want her here. Hear me? I don't want her comin' back here." She signed the paper with a shaky scrawl then stepped back from the door. "We live our lives peaceful-like out here. Don't ask nothin' of nobody, and don't expect nothin' in return. Don't want that child around here, either. You understand me? She's yours now, and I don't care what you do with her so long as she don't go showin' up on my doorstep again." With that, Gertrude stepped back into the shadows of her trailer and disappeared from view.

"I'm not sure what comes next," Alain said.

"Well, I think she just gave you a child."

They stepped off the wooden porch and started down the cluttered path toward the road. "She'll be better off," Alain said, hoping if he said it with enough resolution he might actually begin to believe it.

"She will," Maggie agreed. "And look, I know this isn't what you bargained for, but I'll help you with her until a better situation can be found."

Alain laughed apprehensively. "Look at us, suddenly parents."

"For a day or two."

"She wanted Lilly out of there. I think that's why she sent her to us. To get her out of that situation and hope we'd find something better for her."

"Well, she didn't hesitate to sign the papers. That's for sure."

"We do need to get her to a pediatrician as soon as possible."

"I'll give my mother a call. Back in the day, before she was an administrator, she was a pediatrician. Maybe she'll have time in the next couple of days."

They were most of the way back to the car when Gertrude Aucoin caught up to them. "Thought you should have these," she said, shoving a shoebox into Alain's hands. "They're what came with the kid when she got dropped off. I expect they have information you might want to know."

"What happened to her mother?" Maggie asked.

"Drug overdose."

"And her father?"

"Got himself killed selling drugs on the street. My Joe and I don't have much, not enough to spread around to a third mouth. We didn't want the kid in the first place, and they told us it was only temporary. But that was four years ago, and no one's come to get her. My Joe gets aw-fully…frustrated. He keeps telling me she's not his problem to take care of and that I got to fix things."

"So you sent her to us?" Alain asked.

"Saw you there the other day when I was walkin' by. You looked all official in that white coat and I thought to myself that you could help her. I was right. You will."

"I appreciate your honesty, Mrs. Aucoin," he said as she started to back away. After that, there was nothing left to say. The authorities would do what they needed to, as would he. Which was driving off and putting this incident behind him. So he and Maggie climbed into the car and sped away, glad to be gone from there, glad there had been no confrontation.

On the contrary, he felt some sympathy for Gertrude, in spite of the fact that she was as much a part of Lilly's condition as was her hus-band. The thing was, it was her choice. It wasn't Lilly's, though. And that was what he kept reminding himself as they headed back to Big Swamp, a place where he was going to take on the temporary duties of daddy, it seemed.

"It's a good thing," Maggie reassured him as they puttered along the road without the same sense of urgency they'd felt on their way there.

"I know it is, but what about Lilly? She's been disrupted from her living situation twice in six years now, and I sure as hell don't like pulling the rug out from underneath her again."

"She was being neglected there, Alain. Mistreated and neglected."

"Which justifies removing her, and I don't feel bad about that. But she's going to have to make an adjustment to staying with me for a while then another adjustment when she's sent to a foster situation, and another when she's placed in an adoptive home. And who knows how many more placements will come in between those steps?"

"But she'll be safe, and that's the important thing."

"Maybe it is, but I still feel bad for her."

"We both do," Maggie said solemnly. "We both do."

CHAPTER FOUR

"SO THIS IS the situation. We can take her into custody immediately, but we don't have a family to place her with, and I don't know when one will become available. It could be days or weeks or even longer. The younger children who need pretty much total care always have first priority on our placements, and unfortunately Lilly doesn't fit in as one of the younger children, meaning that she's able to care for herself independently, which puts her in the position of having to go to one of our residential care facilities."

Karen White of the child welfare division was a kind woman, but businesslike. With her plain brown hair pulled tightly into a knot at the nape of her neck, and a thick bone structure that accentuated highly defined cheekbones, she looked as formidable as she was. Alain understood that with a job like hers she had to be formidable, as she was dealing with the lives of innocent children, trying to do what was best for all of them. It had to be tough, but it did bother him that at the end of this particular transaction was a little girl for whom he felt particularly responsible. "Residential care, as in how many children?"

"Forty, maybe more, depending on where we can find her a bed."

His first night with Lilly had been uneventful. Maggie had stayed over, cooked dinner, and everyone had gone to bed early. Poor Lilly simply accepted what was happening to her, no questions asked, no resistance put up. But she did like the clothes Charles Doucet had brought out for her...especially liked the brand-new stuffed teddy bear with the big pink bow he'd given her. Most of all, Alain believed Lilly liked being clean. More than once he'd caught her looking at herself in the mirror and smiling. A child like that, so fragile and vulnerable, didn't need to be warehoused with forty other children.

"And there's no way to get her an individual family any sooner?"

"Never say never in my job, Doctor, but as much as I'd like to be an optimist, I've been at this a long, long time and my gut instinct tells me that Lilly might not find placement at all, because she is able to be independent as far as her daily living skills are concerned. That puts her way ahead of many of our children."

She glanced at Maggie, who was fixing tea for the three of them. "I'm sorry, but this is an area where I can't play favorites, not even for old friends. Every child is equally as deserving of a good placement, and as much as I'd like to see that happen, it doesn't always work out the way we want it to. For now, Lilly will have to be assigned to a care facility rather than a private home."

"I understand," Maggie said, as she poured the brew into three mugs and carried them over to the kitchen table. "But I'm disappointed, because Lilly deserves better than residential care.

Especially after all she's been through…and I'll bet we don't even know the half of it."

"They all do," Karen said. "And we do our best with what's available to us. But what's available is limited."

"So in the meantime…" Alain started, then paused. This was where he was going to step in and do the kind of thing that always got him into trouble or broke his heart. Or both. "Is the document her aunt signed enough to allow Lilly to stay with me until your department can figure out what to do with her?"

"You'd keep her?" Karen asked, sounding quite surprised.

"I'd keep her. We're set up for a child here already…. I'm staying here temporarily, by the way. And I think I can count on one or two of the locals to help watch her while I'm working. So while this isn't exactly the most ideal situation, I think it would be better than sending her into residential care, where I'm afraid she'll get lost."

"We don't lose children," Karen said.

"I know you don't. But children can lose themselves, and Lilly is…very defeated right now. I think an individual situation would work out best for her."

"Plus, you'll have me here part time," Maggie added.

Karen arched speculative eyebrows. "Since when did you become mother material? I remember once, a long time ago, you told me you didn't want to be involved in all that kind of domestic stuff, that you were quite happy to be a professional woman, skip the husband and family."

"That doesn't mean that I don't like children. Just ask my niece, Leonie. We have a lot of fun together."

Karen laughed. "I'm talking long term. A few minutes here and there don't count."

"You make me sound like an ogre," Maggie accused.

"Not an ogre. Just someone who doesn't wear the domestic mantle very well. The good thing, though, is that you know your limitations. So many of the children in our system are the victims of parents who don't recognize their limitations before they do something that's regrettable."

"You make it sound like I'd be one of those who'd keep a child in squalor or abuse them," Maggie argued, not at all happy to be characterized this way, especially in front of Alain.

Sure, she had some qualms about typical domesticity, and maybe she'd said, once upon a time, that she'd never get herself hooked up that way. But she was older now, had seen more of life. Some of her ideals had changed—one of those being her thoughts on one of the things she'd most disliked when she'd been younger. For some reason, it bothered her, letting Alain know that side of her had ever existed.

"Actually, I know you wouldn't. But you'd never allow yourself to be put into a situation where you might feel trapped enough to do the things some people do," Karen said.

No, she wasn't at all happy with this characterization. Especially when she saw the questioning look Alain was giving her. What must he think of her? And how could she defend herself without coming off as looking too defensive, as defensive was often equated to guilty? So rather than standing up for herself, Maggie plastered a smile to her face, took a step back and waited until Karen had gone before she let go and kicked the door shut behind her. Kicked it hard. Put a lot of foot into that kick.

Alain laughed. "If she's a friend, I'd hate to see how your enemies would treat you."

"Years ago, when we were in school, I was more like the person she was talking about. Wanted no part of the perceived establishment. I mean, I had come out of a lot of domesticity that practically overwhelmed me, and I didn't want to surround myself with it. At least, not at that point. But people change. And while maybe I don't come by a domestic or motherly side as naturally as some of the women in my family do, that doesn't mean I don't know how to be domestic or motherly, or can't figure it out. I'm a nurse after all. A caregiver. And I think I'm pretty good at that."

"From what I've seen, you're a damn fine nurse. But in the case of being domestic, there's nothing wrong with being more professional than domestic," Alain said. "My mother was older when she had me and she gave up a brilliant career as an educator to stay home and raise me. I don't think it ever completely fulfilled her, though. I know she wanted to teach but my father was pretty overbearing about having a full-time mother in the house, and I don't think she ever knew she could have both her career and her family. That was another time, and today... there are a lot of choices available to work it out one way or another. Choices my mother never had.

"So you don't have to defend yourself, however you want to be. At least, not with me. Because I believe people should do whatever makes them happiest. Life's short, you know? Why waste it doing something you don't want to?"

"I appreciate that, Alain. I really do. Spoken by the woman whose family is the perfect example of everybody doing what makes them happy. Anyway, speaking of you…I finally got that call from my law firm, and they've agreed to represent you in trying to get the charges of malpractice dropped. I'm the investigator they've assigned, since I'm the one who brought the case. Although you will have to meet with one of our attorneys before we can get anything formal started. So I've agreed to an appointment tomorrow morning, if that works for you."

"What about coverage here? I've got a couple of patients who said they might stop by. Nothing definite, but I'd hate to miss them if they do come in."

"I'll see if my dad can come out for a couple of hours. I'm sure he'll want to watch Lilly for us, and maybe he can bring Leonie for her to play with. And in the meantime…I do have to get back to town this afternoon. I have a client to meet, and I've got to pull a split shift at the hospital this evening. So will you and Lilly be okay out here by yourself, or would you rather bring her back to town, where Justin and Mellette and my parents can help watch her?"

The idea of looking after Lilly all by himself had never really crossed his mind. Somehow, when he'd made the decision to keep her, Maggie had been in that picture. Admittedly, now that Maggie was going to take an exit, it made him nervous. "I may bring her to town for dinner, and I'd like to stop by my house and grab a few personal items, but we'll be fine."

"Well, the Doucet family will be at your disposal, if you need them. You know that, don't you, Alain?"

If he needed them… It was good to know, even though he intended on seeing this temporary father thing through on his own. "Thanks for the offer, and for making me an incidental member of the family. But I think we'll be able to get along on our own." If he could figure out what to do with a little girl.

As it turned out, the hours of the day ticked by faster than he'd expected. Lilly played quietly in the play yard built for Leonie while patients wandered in and out, and he kept her close by while he switched from doctor to carpenter mode and worked on the expansion project. In fact, he even gave Lilly a hard hat and let her carry his tools and assist in other ways where she could be safe. What he noticed was that she was a very dutiful, very hard worker. And so serious about everything. It almost broke his heart she was so serious—a little girl who had known no joy in her life.

He did want to change that for her, so after his day's activities were over, he gathered Lilly up and took her to town to shop for little-girl things…depending on the good grace of the store clerks to guide him through the task of what a child her age needed. More than that, what a child her age should have. And even though he didn't have a lot of cash to put into the effort, he did manage a stack of nice toys and games and an armload of practical clothes. None of which elicited the least little bit of excitement or happiness out of Lilly.

On impulse, he stopped in at a quick-cut shop and got her tangled mess of hair evened out, and while he couldn't tell if Lilly was enjoying the pampering, he did see that she wasn't afraid of having someone give her that kind of attention, either. And afterward he did notice Lilly looking at herself in the mirror with a kind of distant amazement as she studied her features—studied them like she'd never really seen herself before. While she didn't smile, he did see a spark of life in her eyes...and that was encouraging. He was getting through. Which meant a lot. A whole lot.

"Care for some ice cream?" he asked her.

"Ice cream?"

"You know, chocolate, or vanilla, or strawberry?"

She shrugged her tiny shoulders and seemed to retreat back into herself. Did the child not know what ice cream was? Had she never had it? "It's very good," he said. "Sweet and cold."

"I like sweet," she said so shyly she could barely be heard.

"Then ice cream it will be." On impulse, he called Charles Doucet, who was only too happy to bring Leonie and join them.

"How's Mellette?" Alain asked once they were standing in line for ice cream.

"Resting, and not happy about staying down as much as she has to. But Justin's riding herd on her, and she's just going to have to sit it out much more than she'd used to until she's ready to deliver. Good catch on the preeclampsia, by the way."

"Well, once upon a time that's what I did."

"And Maggie tells me she's on your case now, so that means you'll be doing it again pretty soon. Although I understand you're a pretty good handyman, which is just as impressive as being a good obstetrician."

"Jack-of-all-trades."

For Lilly's introduction to ice cream he chose a bowl of plain vanilla with colorful sprinkles, and the girl dug in like it was the best thing she'd ever eaten. Who knew? Maybe it was.

After ice cream, they took the girls to a nearby park, where three-year-old Leonie knew exactly how to play, and poor Lilly seemed at a loss what to do with something as simple as a swing.

"I don't think she's ever been to a park," Alain commented to Charles. "In fact, I don't think she's ever done much of anything other than being a slave to those people."

"Well, my granddaughter is a little livewire. Bring Lilly around often enough, and Leonie will teach her what little girls do. Speaking of which, why don't you leave her with me tonight, and I'll take both girls out to the clinic in the morning? That way you don't have to worry about getting her ready first thing when you need to be getting ready for your appointment."

"Then I could just stay in town tonight, which would make it easier," Alain said.

"And it will give Lilly more time to play with Leonie."

"Are you sure you don't mind doing this? Because Lilly and I would be fine out in Big Swamp tonight, or even in my house, which isn't set up for a child but will suffice."

"She's not a problem to any of us, son." Charles patted Alain on the back. "What's important is you getting to that appointment on time in the morning. My Maggie's looking forward to working on your case, so you want to make sure you make the best impression on her boss as it's her reputation on the line."

"Well, I wouldn't want to do anything to hurt her reputation," he said as they walked over to the sandbox, where Leonie was building a sand-castle and Lilly was watching intently, studying Leonie's every move. "As long as Lilly's okay with the plan…" He bent down. "How would you like to spend the night with Leonie? That will give you the opportunity to play more with her. Then in the morning Dr. Doucet can take you back to Big Swamp, and I'll see you there about lunchtime. Maybe I'll even bring pizza."

"Pizza?" she asked. "Is that like ice cream?"

"No, sweetheart, it isn't. It's like…" He wasn't sure how to describe pizza. "It's like the best food you're ever going to eat." There were so many things to teach her, so many things he wanted her to know, to experience. The thing was, he wanted to be part of that experience. Wanted to be the one to open up a world of firsts for her.

"Pizza's good," she conceded somberly.

"So it's okay if you spend the night here, and I see you tomorrow?"

Lilly nodded, and as she did so little Leonie quietly slipped her hand into Lilly's. New friends. Such a simple thing caused a lump to form in Alain's throat. He really wanted to give Lilly a hug before he left, but she wasn't ready for that. He was, though. Except this wasn't about him. And as he drove away from the park, and left Lilly standing there with Charles and Leonie, he felt the sting of missing Lilly before he was a block away.

"My dad told me about the change in plans, and as this is just a few blocks from the hospital…" She handed him a bag full of cardboard cartons, and the smell of the various mixes of Chinese foods made him aware of just how hungry he was. "I'm assuming you like Chinese. And that you've probably forgotten to eat."

It was after ten, and he'd been working on the entryway to his aunt's house, sanding off old paint and wallpaper, for hours. "Love it."

"Beautiful house," she said, looking around at the scaffolding in place.

"Potential to be beautiful. With a lot of hard work."

"That's how you view life, isn't it?" Maggie

asked as she ran her fingertips lightly over some exposed plaster. "With potential?"

He shrugged. "When you're pretty much tapped out, the way I am, that's all there is."

"I like the optimism." She looked straight at him, appraised the plaster dust in his hair, the hole in his T-shirt exposing just a peek of his chest, the bare feet. "You'll need it for the fight ahead of you, Alain. Winning a malpractice case is never easy, because the public in general is geared to believe that doctors gouge their patients. You'll be fighting a preconceived idea that has nothing at all to do with your case."

"And you're telling me this the night before your firm officially commits to representing me?"

"Just trying to be honest with you." She grabbed a container of egg rolls along with the sweet-and-sour sauce, then smiled. "Now, where do we sit to eat this stuff?"

An hour later, stuffed full of moo goo gai pan, crab won tons, egg foo young and a whole host of other tasty food, Alain retreated to the porch swing, where Maggie joined him. "You have an early-morning appointment, too," he reminded her, stifling a yawn.

"Three hours of sleep, and I'm good to go."

"I used to be that way, back in med school. Then my body protested, or maybe I just got too old to keep up the routine."

"So you're telling me to leave?" she asked him.

"Not so much telling as suggesting that if you want me to be at my best tomorrow…"

"Okay, okay," she said, laughing. "I'm out of here."

"Said the pretty girl to the really stupid doctor," he muttered.

"Said the wise man to the night owl," she responded. Then headed out to her car.

Alain followed and opened the door for her, and for a moment it seemed as if a kiss would be the next logical step. Too logical, too easy. Too tempting under the big, bright moon. So Maggie was the one who forced herself back to reality.

He was her client, that was all. And she had to keep it that way. "See you in the morning, and don't be late," she said, backing away from him. "My boss judges a person on punctuality."

"I'll be on time," he said, taking his own step back, as if he'd just realized the same thing as Maggie. "Drive carefully," he said as he shut the car door after her.

And in a flash she was gone, and he was kicking himself for asking her to leave. But damn, this hadn't been a date, and she'd had no intention of staying over. Still, he didn't feel good about what he'd just done. Maybe because Maggie had suddenly become his lifeline—a lifeline he hadn't known he needed.

Jean-Pierre Robichaud decided to take the lead on Alain's case. He was an impressively large man, with dark chocolate skin, short gray hair and a deep baritone voice that drew attention even if he was only reciting the alphabet. Jean-Pierre had the experience necessary to win the very toughest cases. In point, he hadn't lost a case in over a decade. "You have a very impressive background, young man," Jean-Pierre began the meeting by saying. "Good work history, excellent military history…" He riffled through the pile of papers in front of him for a moment, then looked up at Alain. "Fighting cases like this one is not easy, regardless of the circumstances. But I don't think you deserve being destroyed for something you didn't have any control over.

"So, with the approval of this firm, we've agreed to represent you, and while we know your finances are not in good order, we believe you've paid the price with your military service. Meaning this one is courtesy of the house, Dr. Lalonde. You've done good work for the country, and from what Maggie is telling us, you're doing good work at her family's volunteer clinic."

"I didn't expect this to be pro bono work, sir," Alain responded, not quite sure what to make of the generosity being offered. He was a man who always paid his way, no matter what.

"Don't look the proverbial gift horse in the mouth, young man. It's a simple gesture—nothing unexpected is going to pop out at you later on except maybe a consultation on my niece, who's at the beginning of a very high-risk pregnancy. We may be wanting a second opinion down the line, and it seems high risk is your specialty."

"I can do that," Alain said. "But I won't step on professional toes."

"Didn't expect that you would."

"Well, then, I appreciate what you're offering me."

Jean-Pierre offered him a generous smile. "It's going to be a tough fight, Doctor. Always is under these kinds of circumstances. But our goal here is twofold. First to prove your innocence, then to get your reputation back. It's amazing how even an innocent verdict has a stigma attached to it."

"Once you've been sued—" Alain sighed "—it never goes away, even if the charges are dismissed or the case is won." One of the partners in his medical practice had won the case and lost his career because his patients had no longer trusted him.

"Exactly. But part of what we do is repair that damage, help restore the reputation. That's as important as winning the case. So whatever happens over the next weeks, don't get discouraged. You've got a good case, and we'll prove it. And prove your reputation, as well."

"Again, I appreciate what you're doing."

"Don't thank me. Thank Maggie. Normally we come in at the request of the hospital. In fact, you're the first case we've taken on a personal basis."

"She *is* persuasive, isn't she?" Alain said, looking over at Maggie, who'd been uncharacteristically quiet throughout the meeting.

"Yes, she is when she believes in a good cause. Which is why we hired her and why we're hoping to hang on to her once she gets through law school." Jean-Pierre stood and extended his hand to Alain. "I'll be in touch as soon as I know something. And in the meantime, if you need anything, or can think of anything that should be added to the case, please let Maggie know. Oh, and just to clarify a point, you're not going to countersue in this matter, are you?"

Alain shook his head. "What's the point? It just looks vindictive, and that won't help my reputation. All I want is out from under. A chance to go back to work with my reputation intact."

"Then that's what we'll go for," Jean-Pierre said.

"And what we'll win," Maggie said once they were out the door. "He only takes the biggest cases."

"So why mine? Nothing about this is exactly high profile."

"His son served in Afghanistan a couple of years ago. Was critically wounded, and rescued by a medic who was wounded saving André. Jean-Pierre is as tough as they get in the courtroom—no one I'd ever want to go up against. But he has a soft spot for soldiers."

"Sounds like I've got a damn good team lining up on my side," he said, feeling the first surge of optimism over his future that he'd felt in a long, long time. Thanks to Maggie. "Look, I know it's too early to ask you out for a drink, but would you care to join me for a coffee?"

"Take me someplace where I can get a beignet to go with that and it's a deal. And let me warn you, Alain, I can eat my weight in good beignets."

"I know just the place, down on the riverfront. Want to take a walk or go for a carriage ride?"

"Would you believe that in all the years I've lived here, I've never been on a carriage ride of the city?"

"Have you always been alone? No marriages or near misses?"

"I'm not exactly a socialite, but I'm not a hermit, either. Back when we were kids and my parents gave fabulous parties, my sisters were always trying to find ways to sneak in or to hide somewhere and watch it. I was never that way. Never particularly interested in what went on. Didn't date in high school because I never met a boy who caught my attention. They all seemed sort of silly to me. And I barely dated in college because I was too busy studying and trying to get ahead. You know…multiple goals. Be a nurse, be a lawyer. That takes a lot of time.

"Then in my adult life…" She shrugged. "I suppose that if you don't put the signals out there, or in my case don't know how, no one's going to show much interest. I mean, I've dated, but my dad says I lack the attention span for it. My mother says I'm just too choosy."

"And you?" he asked as he hailed a carriage. "What do you say?"

"Honestly, I don't know. I don't think I've ever met anyone I can see myself with well into my future. And, see, that has to be the thing. My parents have such a good marriage, and if I ever do it, that's what I want. But statistics are against that these days, aren't they? Isn't marriage rated at, like, fifty-fifty? And I don't want one of those *trial* marriages before I do it for real."

"So you just stay away from it altogether?"

"Not altogether. Let's just say I'm judicious. Of course, that leads to spinsterhood, doesn't it?" She smiled. "And I'm very good at that. Not unhappy with it, either."

As the carriage arrived, Alain helped Maggie up and onto the seat and took his place next to her rather than across from her. It was an open carriage, very elegant. White, pulled by a white horse. Maybe something more appropriate for romance, she thought as they ambled their way through the French Quarter, by Jackson Square, with all its statue people and tourists mingling in the street. She especially liked seeing all the beautiful bougainvillea in bloom, draping itself from various doorways. And the wisteria…to die for. Her New Orleans. The reason she could never leave. She loved it all too much. Couldn't imagine her life anywhere else but here.

Using her phone, Maggie snapped multiple pictures of things she'd seen hundreds of times before, but she was a tourist today, getting herself caught up in the festive atmosphere the way most tourists did. Once, when he wasn't looking, she snapped a profile picture of Alain against the backdrop of the President Andrew Jackson statue, then looked at the image on her phone. He was really quite handsome. A veritable prince, riding along in the carriage, looking so regal and in control of himself.

She enjoyed looking at him, from afar, or up close. Liked him best in his low-riding jeans and T-shirt, though, rather than sitting atop a marble horse like President Jackson. The rugged Alain was how she thought of him. He was a real sigh-maker. Of course, he wasn't so shabby in scrubs, or even his gray suit. Truly, he was a man worthy of a second or even a third look, she decided as they clip-clopped along the street and exited the carriage at an open-air café, where she noticed that he was a man who also drew a fair share of admiring glances from other women. And just for this little while, she was the one who had him.

It was a strange sensation, feeling the burst of pride that came from being Alain's girl, even if only for a few moments. One she'd never felt before, not with anyone. One she liked, nevertheless. Liked a whole lot. But it was also a sensation that frightened her, as she knew she might like to be in this very same position again. Maybe she would have under other circumstances.

But he was a client. *Her* client. And the law firm had a very strict policy where members of the firm could not date or otherwise fraternize with clients. One with which she fundamentally agreed. So, while she'd finally found a man who might prove to be more than a casual acquaintance, there was nothing she could do about it. Alain Lalonde was off-limits to her in every way but professional.

After beignets, she told herself. *After beignets.*

CHAPTER FIVE

"WE WENT SHOPPING for some basics and Lilly decided she wants new shoes other than the white sneakers I bought her." White, basic, perfect for everyday wear. "Something frilly that maybe she can wear to a party. She said she's never had anything pretty like the shoes she saw in one of the windows, and she wants a particular pair that has a bow and sparkles. Not just regular sparkles, though. Pink-and-purple sparkles."

Alain took a long drink of water from an aluminum bottle and wiped the sweat from his brow with the back of his arm. So far, he'd had no patients come in today, which worked out well since he was in the middle of setting in new overhead beams that would separate the old clinic from the small minor surgery he was building onto the rear of the building. And nearly exhausting himself doing so for the past six hours, busting himself as hard as he could to get the beginnings of the framing completed.

For once, he truly believed all the different responsibilities he'd taken on were going to be the ruin of him. Carpenter, doctor, father... He knew other men did this day in, day out: worked back-breaking multiple jobs to support a family. Did it with grace and style. And he had all the compassion in the world for them. But he wasn't one of them, and he'd admit it to anyone who was listening, because this was killing him. Physically breaking him down into an exhausted heap, as he wasn't used to it. Knocking him down with every weakness he had, then jamming them in over and over. Sissifying him. Although he sure as hell didn't like admitting he was a sissy.

So he took another drink of water, wiped the sweat off his face yet again and hoisted the shorter of the beams up on his shoulder. "I told her that I couldn't get them for her now, and while she didn't put up a fuss or even complain

a little, the look of disappointment on her face…
Damn, being a father is hard when that's what
you're met with. How did your dad manage with
seven daughters playing on his emotions, and
I'm guessing that was pretty much all the time?"

"First off, he did have help. My dad was the
soft one, my mother much more the one to put
things in proper perspective. As in saying 'No!'
But as far as being daddy to seven girls…I think
with him that practice must have made perfect.
You know, trial and error. Try it out on one, and
if it worked, do it again on another. If it failed,
try something different."

She smiled fondly. "I think he would have wel-
comed seven more girls into the family with
grace and never complained. He's such a…good
man. Nurturing. Caring. Not that my mother
wasn't like that because she was. But she never
let any of us get away with the things Daddy
did, and still doesn't."

"Well, Charles Doucet should write a book on
raising daughters, because I think it could be a

best seller. I know I'd buy it and commit it to memory. And as far as the shoes go…"

"Pink *is* a pretty popular color with girls Lilly's age. I remember I had my own pink stage going on for a few years. Everything I wore had to be pink. My bed was pink, the side of the room I shared with Mellette was all decorated in pink…unlike Mellette, who tormented me with ugly colors like orange and green. On purpose."

"And what did your father do about that?"

Maggie laughed. "Taped a dividing line down the center of the room. Told me I had full control of my side, and Mellette had full control of her side. And the first one who encroached on the other lost all rights to the color scheme and the other one of us could then do the decorating."

"Man's a genius. Pure genius."

"He is. With the patience of a saint because he was the one who took each of us shopping for our color choices. My mother was of a mind to paint everything all white and let us deal with it, but Daddy was into letting us express our creativity."

"And you expressed yours in pink."

Maggie nodded. "As pink as you could make half a room. It was a hideous room, really, and Mellette and I still laugh about it, but at the time it was an important part of our growing up."

"Like pink shoes for a little girl who's probably had no other choices allowed in her life."

"Something like that."

"So now we get down to the other issue. Do you honestly think I look like someone who should go traipsing into a children's store, looking the way I do? Lilly and I went to a discount mart, so it didn't matter that I looked totally out of place in the children's department. But in a frilly little store for little girls?"

She appraised his jeans with holes in the knees, his torn T-shirt, his work boots, his tool belt and hard hat. "You do look a little...rough, now that you mention it."

"Which means the shoes will have to wait.

First, until I have time to go back and buy them. Second, until I can afford them. They cost half as much as the five outfits, shoes and unmentionables I got her at the discount store. And third, I do need to find some kind of courage to get me through those doors because…"

Maggie laughed. "Too frilly for a man of your many talents."

"Would your dad go into a store like that? It had unicorns in the window, Maggie! Pink, blue and purple unicorns."

"He has, and he would."

"Then he's a better man than I am."

"Not better. Just *differently* experienced. You didn't have time to work yourself up to daddyhood. It was just thrust upon you. One day you were single, the next you were…encumbered. But trust me, in time a store like that won't faze you, not even looking the way you look right now." She took a good, hard look at him and curved her lips into a warm smile. "And I'm guessing the store clerks might even appreciate the look. But…until you get comfortable with the concept, I could take her, if you want me to," Maggie said. "And pay for the shoes. It's not a big deal, really."

"For you, maybe it's not a big deal, and I appreciate the offer. But I'm the one raising Lilly right now, and I want to be her provider. She has a roof over her head, friends to play with, she's fed and that's more than she's had before, so the shoes will have to wait."

He stepped sideways then turned to head into the new part of the structure. "And if that seems like I'm being too harsh, I'm sorry, but that's the way it is. Life isn't always fair. It's hardly ever the way you want it to be, either. Especially when pink shoes are involved."

"Spoken like a man who's been beaten down."

"Beaten down more than once. And learned some hard lessons from the experiences."

"Fine, then no shoe arguments from me," Maggie said. "And you're right. What Lilly needs can't be bought. She has everything that's necessary, and the rest of it can come…or not come, depending on what the court decides to do with her. You're doing an amazing thing, taking care of her temporarily, and she's one lucky little girl to have you."

"Speaking of which, I have a hearing tomorrow before the child services judge, if you'd care to come and stand up as a character witness."

"Jean-Pierre already told me, and I've got the time blocked out. Although these hearings are usually pretty cut-and-dried. Each side presents its evidence—our side why the child should stay with you, their side why she shouldn't. And the judge will usually decide based on the preliminary evidence given."

"And my chances?"

"With most lawyers representing you, not good. But Jean-Pierre's appearance in a juvenile hearing will have some impact, so we're pretty hopeful." She reached over and squeezed his arm. "Like I said, the man doesn't lose. Not even in a hearing like this one. But you've got to ask yourself one hard question, Alain. If you win, do you really want to take care of Lilly for what could amount to be a very long time? She's going to be hard to place in the foster system, and equally as hard to adopt because of her age."

"I've thought about it, and I want to do this. That look in her eyes…it's so sad. I know she won't have a traditional lifestyle with me, but I do think I can change that look, maybe show her what it's like to be happy."

"Just like that?" Maggie snapped her fingers. "From carefree bachelor to surrogate father? You make darned sure it's what you want before we get to court, because once that child is placed, she doesn't need another disruption."

"You don't think I can do it?"

"Actually, I think you can. But you're a little down-and-out yourself right now and I wonder if that's what's pulling you in Lilly's direction. It's a valid consideration."

"Valid, maybe. But that's not me, Maggie. If I make the commitment, I stay with it."

"Trust me, Alain. Taking care of Lilly is about much more than honoring a commitment. Think about it. That's all I'm saying. You have until tomorrow and nobody's going to think less of you if you decide it's a responsibility you don't want or can't handle."

He drew in a sharp breath. "I can do this," he said, trying to hold back his temper. Because this conversation was making him angry. Maybe he didn't have a clear-cut picture on why he wanted to become guardian to that little girl, and maybe to an outsider it didn't look like a good choice. But the fact remained that he did want her. No matter what, he wanted to give that little girl proper care until a family could be found for her. And maybe it was as simple as his mother, who always made room at the dinner table for anyone who needed a meal, or who'd offered a bed to virtual strangers who'd fallen on hard times.

Or maybe it was even simpler. He'd looked into Lilly's eyes and seen her soul—a good soul, a soul that hadn't given up, in spite of her circumstances. Whatever the case, he was sure. "It's what I want."

"Then good luck," she said, and stepped back as Alain handed the beam off to two workers and stepped aside as they lifted it into place. Then he pulled the drill off his tool belt while they steadied the beam in place for him to fasten to the support beams. "Oh, and it would be nice having you sitting there *on my side,* without the skepticism. Sometimes it feels like the whole deck is stacked against me and I don't want part of my legal team helping stack that deck."

"Not the deck, Alain. Just a couple of cards in it maybe, but not the full fifty-two."

"Well, if the majority of the fifty-two weren't tilting against me, I'd be back home, practicing medicine, instead of being in Big Swamp, trying to build a clinic for someone else to practice medicine."

"Give it time," she consoled.

"Time, I've got. And that's about all I've got."

He screwed another few bolts into the wood, then stepped back to appraise his work. "It's beginning to look like what it's supposed to be," he said with some pride as he glanced across to the enclosed play yard as Mrs. Dolly Tremaine brought Lilly outside for some afternoon exercise. The people here were so good to him, a virtual stranger, helping him out the way they were. People to trust, he decided. People he liked. "And I'm hoping that inside two months it can be used as a minor surgical suite without collapsing the way my life seems to be."

"Want me to swing from your rafters in order to prove they won't fall down?" she offered.

"That's displaying an awful lot of trust. Foolish trust, if you ask me."

"But you've built before, haven't you?"

"One of the many things I did to get myself through school."

"So you know what you're doing." Statement, not question.

"Up to a point."

Maggie laughed. "Hoist me up, let me prove it."

"No way in hell I'm going to let you swing from my rafters. If anyone's going to do it…"

With that, Alain pulled himself up on the beam and did several chin-ups. Quite successfully. Nothing budged. Nothing fell down.

And Maggie fanned herself, watching all that brawn flexing itself. "Not bad," she finally managed to say. And she didn't mean the chin-ups.

"Not bad? That's it?"

"Um, makes a respectable frame for a surgery. Especially if any of the patients who come in here want to do chin-ups."

"Very funny," he said, lowering himself back down then dropping to the ground.

"If you have a sense of humor," she teased.

It was an obvious flirt. Even he, as oblivious as he was to most things, could feel it. But what he didn't know was if she was responding to his flirting or he to hers. Whichever the case, the last thing he needed was to add one more complication to his life. Especially a complication that came in the form of one of his legal representatives. Conflict of interest, no doubt. That had been a rule between members of his medical practice and patients, and he was sure it had to be a rule between members of the legal practice and clients.

Still, he liked the flirting. What man wouldn't? "Think your sister will approve of everything we're doing here?"

"Mellette really *did* want to be around for more of this," Maggie said. "She's so invested in the changes, and I know it's got to be frustrating her that she can't be out here, overseeing everything. She's really take-charge that way."

"And you're not? Working as a nurse, working for a law firm, going to law school in your spare time, all with the goal of commingling your medical and legal careers."

"That's different."

Alain laughed. "How?"

She thought for a minute, then laughed with

him. "Okay, so maybe my sister and I are alike in some ways."

"Aggressive girls," he commented.

"Which I'll take as a compliment. And thank you for my sister as well, because she'd take that as a compliment, too."

"How's Mellette doing, by the way?"

"Resting comfortably. Physically comfortably, anyway. Emotionally, she's pretty miserable, though."

"That's understandable, especially when someone who doesn't like being kept down is being kept down." Alain laughed. "I've had a lot of patients just like her, who once they hold that new baby in their arms for the first time forget everything else that came before. Mellette's going to be that way, just wait and see. Once she delivers a beautiful, healthy baby, everything will be better. Anyway, does she know if it's a boy or a girl? I'm guessing a girl, since she's carrying it spread out. Boys carry more like a basketball." He indicated a ball-shaped belly.

"Old wives' tale," Maggie said. "Same as if you tie your wedding band to a string and hold it over a pregnant belly. If it goes in circles it's a boy. If it goes from side to side it's a girl." She laughed. "Folk medicine does have some basis in truth, which is part of what we practice at Eula's House, but not in predicting pregnancy."

"Maybe you're right, maybe you're not. My grandmother claimed she always got the gender right. If it's a tight little ball up front it's a boy, if it spreads out all the way around it's a girl. She swore by it, and her patients swore by her predictions."

"Was your grandmother a doctor?"

"A trained nurse and midwife with lots of practical experience taught her by her mother, who had no formal training. They lived in a small community, not unlike Big Swamp, and the women of my family were the ones who did all the birthing. My grandmothers on my dad's side as far back as the genealogy goes. I think that's the reason I chose obstetrics, because I was always amazed when my grandmother walked into the bedroom empty-handed, and a little while later came out with a squirming, crying, brand-new baby."

"You really liked that?" Maggie asked.

"Actually, at first it creeped me out, hearing all that screaming and shouting coming from the other room during the birthing process. She had a birthing room in her house…a house with very thin walls. And if I was staying there and one of the women actually came there to give birth, I'd hide under my grandma's bed, put my baseball mitts over my ears.

"Then one day my grandma asked me to come in and help her. It was a breech birth, twins. She had me pushing down on the woman's fat belly, sort of turning the baby, as I recall. And I could feel the babies in there, alive, trying to get out. Grandma got them turned easily enough, and I saw, for my very first time, a real live birth. It was messy, it about made me sick at my stomach, but there were two little girls who'd just come into the world with my help and…"

"And you were hooked."

Alain smiled. "Hooked, end of story. After that, it's all I wanted. Anyway, my parents were teachers, so we weren't rich, but they put away every spare penny they could save to get me to medical school. And that's the end of my story. Except the part where they don't know their years of scrimping didn't pan out."

"But you took a tour in the military. Why'd you do that?"

"A hitch in the military helped offset some of my school expenses, and I stayed long enough to get all the education I needed."

"And your parents and grandmother?"

"Parents retired from teaching, grandmother was a midwife until she was about ninety. She's gone now."

"And your grandmother's percentages on predicting the gender?"

"Always right, as far as I know. Or if she'd been wrong, I've never been told."

"Are your percentages that good in your obstetrics practice? Because Mellette did have an ultrasound, and it's a girl."

"Old wives' tale," Alain said, as he motioned Maggie back from the O.R.-to-be and pulled out his hammer. "It never let my grandma down. Me, I prefer an ultrasound. That, and Justin already mentioned it to me."

It had been a while since he'd dressed in a suit, and while the necktie wasn't exactly choking him, he sure wasn't feeling easy about things, and it had nothing to do with the charcoal-gray suit he was wearing, or the black oxfords that pinched his feet. Dear Lord, how had he dressed like this on a daily basis? In such a short time he'd become accustomed to a more casual approach to life, and he liked it so much better. But court protocol being what it was called for a more formal version of Dr. Alain Lalonde, and that was what he was about to give them, as Lilly's future did matter that much to him.

He'd tossed and turned all night thinking about it, thinking how it would be easier to simply walk away and let Child Services do what they wanted. But he'd tucked the little girl into bed this evening and read her a bedtime story, and she'd been so eager to hear another one. She couldn't wait until tomorrow night.

Nobody had ever read to that child before, and it was such a simple thing. And maybe that was what convinced him more than anything that he wanted to win this fight—he wanted to read to her, and show her things she'd never seen before. Take her to zoos. And museums. Open new doors...doors every child deserved to have opened.

True to his word, Jean-Pierre, who'd agreed to handle this matter, met Alain outside the court-room door the next afternoon, with only moments to spare before they entered the chambers. And unlike what Alain had expected—probably a TV version of a courtroom with massive mahogany wall panels, some kind of overhead gallery and enough seats to fit hundreds of spectators, this room was small, no room for a jury box and only two rows of seats for spectators.

The plaintiff and defendant tables were nothing more than what you'd see in a dated library, and the chairs were so straight-backed they were uncomfortable. To top it off, the room was dim and musty, its windows tinted over in a yellowish paint. And the judge's bench was little more than a standard library tables, like theirs was.

Alain felt mildly overdressed for the room, actually. But it didn't matter, because he was about to be judged on everything he said or did— judged and condemned or judged and approved.

"Let me do the talking unless you are specifically addressed," Jean-Pierre Robichaud cautioned him as they took their place at the table. "And quit looking so miserable. This is only a preliminary hearing, and it has nothing to do with the malpractice claims against you. If they do ask you anything about that, which they shouldn't but they might, for God's sake keep your mouth shut!"

"And, please, look pleasant," Maggie said, as she slipped into the chair on the other side of him. "Right now you look like you're about to be lynched."

"This is my first time…" Alain explained.

"Well, with what you've got coming up in the future, you'd better get used to it, because there's a whole lot more of this down the line." She gave his hand a squeeze then loosened his tie for him. "Better. Now sit back and watch Jean-Pierre work his magic."

"Are you sure you want to take custody of the child?" Jean-Pierre whispered to Alain. "It's an odd circumstance at best, and no one would bat an eyelid if you changed your mind and walked away from this. I mean, there are no blood ties, not even a former acquaintanceship."

"I worked in squalor in Afghanistan, saw and worked with kids like Lilly every day, and couldn't do a damn thing but bandage their wounds. I volunteered at an orphanage, and nothing I did for those kids made a real difference, but this time I can make that difference. And I want to."

"I didn't know that about you," Maggie whispered.

"There are lots of things you don't know about me," Alain said.

"But I'll find out the further we get into the malpractice investigation, correct? Because there's going to come a time when you can't keep secrets from me." She gave him a suspicious look, one that showed she knew there was more underneath Alain's rugged surface than he let on. "And you do have them, don't you, Alain?"

He glanced over at her, gave her a curious look, one that couldn't be interpreted, and nodded. "If you have to, that's what we'll do." Secrets from so long ago, buried in a court archive that was sealed. He wasn't sure he was ready to go there again, because he believed his past was buried deep enough. But who knew?

"I have to," she said, "if you want to win your malpractice case. Jean-Pierre and I can't afford secrets coming out at the wrong time. Not knowing is what can lose us our case."

Knowing could cost him his case, as well. So apparently his choice was to roll the dice and see how lucky, or unlucky, he was. And he did always have his carpentry to fall back on if his medical practice was taken away. "Okay, I have a juvenile record. Spent about a year being resentful because my parents were too old, and I did things like shoplifting, joyriding in a stolen car. I was a pretty good graffiti artist, too. Paid with two years of after-school and every weekend labor in a nursing home when I got caught."

Maggie laughed. "I already knew that. I called your school to check you out—part of my investigation—and let's just say that the records they read me were not glowing."

"Do you know about the scar on my hind end?"

"Cleats, when you were playing football in college."

"I had a hernia operation, too."

"Quite successfully." She smiled. "And the nursing notes showed you were a very impatient patient."

"Is there anything you didn't discover about me in your research?"

"Maybe a couple of things, but give me time. I'll come up with them."

"Why do I feel...violated?" he grumbled.

"You're going to be damned grateful for her skills one day, young man," Jean-Pierre said. "She's the best."

"Or the nosiest," Alain grumbled again, then became quiet when the social services representatives entered en masse and took a seat at the opposite table.

One attorney—a formidable-looking woman named Alvira Devereaux, a blonde, mid-thirties man-killer in looks and also by reputation; a social services representative named

Olive Olivette, a gray-haired sixtyish woman who looked beleaguered and too tired to care; a young girl named Crystal, who was all shiny eyed and eager, which gave her away as an intern or new hire, as her only job seemed to be to carry the file folder.

One thing for sure, in appraising them they all seemed primed and ready to present their case. And Alain didn't like that one little bit. Over the course of his teen years he'd been in this position too many times, all on the wrong side, facing prosecutors like them. Or more like getting whipped by prosecutors like them while he was being represented by an overworked court appointee who couldn't even remember his name.

Long story short, he wasn't used to winning, wasn't used to being on the side where right and justice and a whole lot of mercy triumphed. Which gave him no confidence whatsoever at this hearing. And who the hell had called it a hearing anyway, when by all intents and purposes it was a trial, with him being placed on the hot seat and examined for his worthiness to take care of a child.

"Formidable representation," the attorney sitting across from leaned forward and said. She was a curvy woman with long black hair pulled back into a braid, and she wore a red skirt that seemed much too small and tight for the occasion, in Alain's opinion. It would have been more appropriate in a bar, after work, over drinks, where the appreciative stares might have been more appropriate. But what he noticed was that under the table, when she crossed her legs, her skirt rode up even higher, barely covering half her thigh. A sight that was definitely not overlooked by the judge, who entered the courtroom without a robe, feasted his eyes, nodded at the group, then took his seat.

Alvira Devereaux knew her way around, Alain decided. And she used it to her advantage. While Maggie was dressed in a sensible, knee-length navy skirt, white blouse, and jacket to match the skirt. Prim and proper.

He sure hoped prim and proper could win the race, because the judge had yet to take his gaze off Alvira Devereaux.

Alain gulped audibly as Judge Henri Breaux began, "This is an informal hearing. Nothing more, nothing less. We're simply here to determine the better short-term care of the child Lilly Anna Montrose, who was removed from her custodial caregivers, her biological aunt and non-biological uncle."

The judge's eyes skimmed over the red skirt yet again, then fixed on Jean-Pierre. "It's an honor to have you in our courtroom today, Mr. Robichaud. We don't often have a person of your reputation and prestige represented here."

"It's my pleasure to be here, Your Honor," Jean-Pierre said, his voice as smooth as melting butter, even though the look on his face was clear disapproval over the way Judge Breaux was drooling over the red skirt. "It's a clear-cut case where the aunt has granted custody, and since Social Services have seen fit to challenge that,

I should think we can dispatch with the matter quickly and fairly since it's all laid out before you in precise legal terms."

The judge nodded then glanced down at the papers. "And what say you, Miss Devereaux?" he asked the opposing attorney.

"What we contend, Your Honor, is that Dr. Lalonde is neither fit nor proper to care for a young child, especially given his circumstances."

"His circumstances?" the judge asked, then looked directly at Alain. "And what would those be, sir?"

"Another legal matter about which we are not prepared to disclose any information in an open situation that has yet to have its day in court, your honor," Jean-Pierre answered. "My client is here today based only on the matter before us, and it is not my intention to allow him to be tried, or even heard, on any other matter.

"Now, I do have to advise the court that I am prepared to present Mrs. Gertrude Aucoin, the aunt to Lilly Montrose, who is ready to testify that she has watched Dr. Lalonde from afar for quite a while and decided, based on what she saw, she wanted him to raise the girl. It would take a postponement and sufficient time to serve a subpoena, which I can and will do, if the court so pleases." He paused for effect then continued. "Mrs. Aucoin is in a delicate living situation herself and I'd prefer not to make that any more complicated than it already is, but if I have to…"

"Witness notwithstanding, Your Honor, there is another circumstance that should be brought to your attention."

"Moral turpitude in question, Miss Devereaux?'

"No, sir, but…"

"Prior convictions or even arrests on suspicion of child crimes?"

"No, your honor, but if you'll allow me to explain?"

"Does this explanation have any legal bearing on this case, and this case only?"

"Can I approach the bench?" Alvira finally asked.

The judge signaled them both forward, and as they went, Alain leaned over to Maggie. "So what's this about?"

"She's trying to get your existing malpractice suit entered as proof that you're not fit to take care of Lilly."

"Yet I've delivered successfully in hundreds of high-risk pregnancies," he snapped. "Maybe I should go up there and tell him that."

"Look, Jean-Pierre knows what he's doing. Trust him."

"It's hard to trust anyone, especially the red skirt with the wiggle that the judge can't take his eyes off."

"Neither can you," Maggie teased.

"That's beside the point."

"Is it? Even Jean-Pierre, the most devoted husband in the world, is having a look. But those kinds of tactics fall short in the courtroom. The judge has seen it all before, and I mean *all*.

Miss Devereaux is obviously new to this, she doesn't have her courtroom style down yet, and while she may be impressing a few of the men here, she's not impressing the legal system, and that's what you need to trust more than anything else."

"You don't dress like that for court. In fact, you're dressed rather…plainly." And in her case plain was definitely sexy.

"I don't even own anything like that."

"Too bad," Alain quipped as Jean-Pierre headed back to the table. He gave Alain a half smile, then sat down, adjusting his massive form into the uncomfortable chair.

"We're good" was all he said as Miss Devereaux yanked at her skirt, trying to pull it lower than the lack of fabric in it would allow it to go.

"So, Dr. Lalonde, your petition would give you custody of Lilly until such a time that she could be placed in a proper foster home. And according to Child Services, they can't specify a time when they can find that home for her, given that she's older, their foster-care system is in need of more caregivers and that younger or dependent children always get the available slots. I believe that about sums it up."

"Yes, it does," Jean-Pierre said, in Alain's stead.

"Also, according to our disclosure, you're not only working as a doctor but you're physically building a clinic addition in Big Swamp, where a number of the local ladies have agreed to look after Lilly during your work hours. I also have letters of endorsement from both Dr. Zenobia and Dr. Charles Doucet, stating that their family is willing to step in and assist you whenever help is required." He glanced at the social services representative. "And you have...nothing substantial to repudiate the letters of endorsement we now have on file. Is that correct?"

"My argument, Judge Breaux, is based on the child services agency contention that having a man stepping in to temporarily raise a young girl is not appropriate."

"Based on what facts?" he asked the attorney.

"Based on appearances, sir."

"Then you would condemn any number of fathers who are raising their daughters without a woman in the house? Or condemning Lilly because she is not a male child? Is that what you're telling me?"

"A father is different," Miss Devereaux continued. "A legal parent is always different. And certainly we're not condemning Lilly because she's a little girl."

The judge sighed audibly. "This child has no legal parent, and she was willingly given away by her guardian. Given into the doctor's care. Which holds merit with this court, Miss Devereaux, even given the circumstances under which this action transpired. Unless you can produce a family I deem worthy to care for Lilly Montrose before I render my judgment, I intend to find for Dr. Lalonde, and thank him for his willingness to step in and do the honorable thing. So do you have someone right now, right this very minute?"

"No, we do not," Miss Devereaux said, her demeanor now taking on defeat. Slumped shoulders, wrinkles creasing her forehead.

"Very well. Then I find that Dr. Lalonde is a suitable guardian for Lilly Anne Montrose until such a time that better arrangements are presented to this court." He banged his gavel, then stood. And this time he didn't so much as glance at Miss Devereaux, who stood, then proceeded to tug her skirt back into its proper place.

"So what did you say to convince him?" Alain asked Jean-Pierre.

"You said it with your high-risk practice. His wife had a high-risk pregnancy, almost lost her baby and her life, and a very good doctor saved them both. He found that the malpractice suit wasn't admissible, as Miss Devereaux had hoped it would be. And while his visual attention might have been more fixed on her legs, his judicial attention was definitely fixed on the case. Oh, and I expect that Miss Devereaux will get an informal letter of reprimand about her appearance in the next day or so." Jean-Pierre smiled. "Henri Breaux is a good representative of the legal system and he doesn't approve of such tactics."

"Too bad he can't hear my malpractice case," Alain said.

"For that, we've drawn Amelia Tassin, I'm afraid."

Maggie audibly gulped. "I've read about her."

"And I take it what you've read isn't good."

"She's fair," Jean-Pierre said, but hesitantly.

"Fair, if she's having a good day. Which she doesn't have many of."

"She will side with the evidence, which we do have to prove our case," Jean-Pierre said.

"And she's chopped at least two inches of height off every lawyer who's ever come before her," Maggie went on. "I've done my homework, and she rarely sides with the doctor."

"But I've done my homework," Jean-Pierre countered, "and I never lose."

"So I'm sensing that Judge Tassin is not a good choice for us."

"She's not a good choice for anybody," Maggie said despondently as they left the courtroom. "I know Jean-Pierre is optimistic, and if anyone can win in Judge Tassin's courtroom, it will be him. But she's been accused of having a bias."

"If we even go to trial," Jean-Pierre said, then smiled.

"What's that supposed to mean?" Alain asked.

"Nothing yet, but Maggie's on your case, and that says a lot."

"Would you have some secrets, Maggie?" Alain teased.

"One or two. And that's all I'm going to say, except that when I have the time I'm going to get Lilly and bring her back to New Orleans. She needs those pink shoes, and she needs them bad!"

He had an idea that it was Maggie who needed the pink shoes far worse than Lilly did. But who was he to argue? In fact, if pink shoes fixed everything, maybe he'd just get himself a pair, too.

CHAPTER SIX

H<small>IS</small> <small>HOUSE</small> <small>WAS</small> really no place for a child to stay, at least not for the long term. Half of it was under dusty sheets and half of it was in renovation, covered in plastic and sawdust. He'd managed to make their sleeping quarters and a corner of the kitchen good for the night, but in the long term it just wasn't the place where he wanted to keep a child.

Only thing was, the sleeping quarters at Eula's House weren't much better. With the exception of the kitchen and the room they used as an exam room, it was a total mess. And like his house, only a couple of rooms remained intact. Oh, and the fenced-in play yard. He'd managed to keep the construction totally away from that.

It was strange how only after he'd been awarded custody had he even begun to think of such things—child safety, child convenience, child comfort. Lucky for him Lilly wasn't a fussy child about anything, which did worry him, as children her age had definite preferences. Or should have preferences. But she simply went along with whatever was put in front of her. Seemed content with what she had but not overjoyed with anything. Which was oddly unsettling.

"Is she better today?" Maggie asked on her way in the clinic door to start the morning shift, whatever that might be, since there were no appointments scheduled on the book. "Now that you've explained to her you'll be keeping her for the next little while, what in the world are you going to do with her?"

"I think she'll be easy enough to have around. I mean, she accepted the judge's decision to let her stay with me pretty much the way she did the white sneakers I bought her. It wasn't her choice, but she was polite about it and that's as far as it went. No opinion expressed, no temper tantrum, no resistance. She merely went along with the decision made for her...I kind of wished she'd expressed something, though. Getting through to Lilly would be good."

"You will. Once she's settled in and knows what to expect, she'll do better."

"I hope so."

Maggie stepped up to Alain, who was standing at the window, watching Lilly and two of her friends play in the yard, and gave his arm a squeeze. "Well, just give it some time. Her entire world is changing, and as bad as the one was from where she came, she's just not sure what to make of the new one. Maybe she doesn't want to get attached. Attachment is a scary thing, you know."

"Why's that?" he asked, as he shrugged into a white lab coat, ready to see patients.

"You get used to something then it's gone, as in taken away from you, and your heart gets broken."

"What did you ever have that was taken away?" he asked.

"An almost fiancé. I found him bland, but bland was safe for me, even though I wasn't quite ready to say yes to a future with him. At the time I was trying to figure out some compromises in my life that would make it all fit together. Then he dumped me, told me I was boring, too much work, not enough fun. Can't say that it broke my heart exactly, but it sure messed me up for a while, seeing myself through someone else's eyes.

"Threw me into the arms of the worst rebound in history…. And the thing I think that broke my heart was that my heart wasn't broken. Made me realize that I was in a place where it was easier to stay…alone."

"Because you couldn't love him enough? I don't think we always have a choice in that. We love whomever we love, and the emotions and motivations directing that are often a mystery that takes a lifetime to unravel."

"But it's a rude awakening, Alain, discovering yourself the way I did. Of course, what came out of that experience is that I know who I am, know what I can and can't do and don't go places I have no place being. Like involved in a relationship. I mean Marc is a good man, to most women he's probably perfect, but I..."

"He wasn't the right man, so you sentence yourself to a life without relationships because of it," he countered gently. "It won't always be that way, especially when the right man comes along."

She nodded. "I think I was combating loneliness with him, and I suppose he knew that all along, or figured it out somewhere along the way. I truly believe he knew exactly where he stood in my life, and that's the worst part. He deserved someone and something better, and all he ended up with was me. Me, Alain! All he got was me."

"Because that's what he wanted, Maggie. He didn't settle. He chose. But you *un*chose for him and pushed him away. See, there's a big difference between choosing and settling. One's dictated by your head and the other is compelled by your heart. He knew you weren't compelled, and that's why he left. I understand that."

"Well, he was right. I wasn't the one for him. After a whole year of dating I couldn't even bring myself to give him an answer when he asked me where we were headed. A *whole* year, and I couldn't figure it out! It was just..."

"Boring."

She shrugged. "Does that make me a terrible person?"

"It makes you human, that's all. But are you going to forever lock yourself away because of that? Because you're just like everybody else and make the wrong choices and decisions sometimes?"

"Well, he did get a nice wife, they have a beautiful child and they're happy. At least it turned out right for one of us."

"So you're done trying?" Alain laughed, but

sadly, in a way that showed he knew, he understood. "And you think you're able to put yourself in the position of trying to be all knowing? You think you should be able to predict life, and futures and outcomes?"

"My life, yes. Because I shape it to be what it should be."

"And what if you fall in love someday? Really in love. In love so much you can't stop it or hold it back or do anything other than let it consume your life. And while I'm not saying this will happen, take me for an example. What if you should fall in love with me?"

Her eyes snapped up at him. "Don't even joke about something like that, Alain. Of course I'm not going to fall in love with you. You're...damaged."

"And you're not?"

"Oh, I'm very damaged. But it's something I can only work through alone. Without help. Without anyone there to show me the way. But the difference between you and me is that I know that. Whereas you have some kind of optimism going on that makes you believe you can make a difference. The truth is, in the end, nobody ever really makes a difference. Not one that affects the whole picture."

"So because you can't affect the big picture, you keep yourself isolated. Change the entire world or change nothing at all."

She brushed back her hair, took a deep breath and fought hard to regain her composure. "That's not fair. I try to make a difference where I can. I volunteer at the clinic, which is helping someone. Plus I work in two careers that help. And I'm not isolated. Just look at me. I have a full life, people coming and going, fulfilling jobs with more on the horizon."

"So, see, you do make a difference. And that affects the big picture, whether or not you can see it. One person taken care of today, another life tomorrow—who's to say how any of those lives will turn out? Who those people will become, or who they'll help along the way? You don't have to see the big picture, Maggie, to be part of it. And as far as more on the horizon, more of what? The things you think you need or the things you really want? Or are you one of those people who can't even admit what you want or need? Not even to yourself?"

"What I want and what I need are more of what I've got. More job. More time to do that job. More opportunities to advance in that job."

"Then 'all job' makes you happy, or is that just a safe place to be?"

She sat down at the breakfast table and poured herself a cup of coffee. It was fresh brewed, smelled, oh, so inviting of chicory and complemented the plate of Annabelle Hawthorne's sweet biscuits she'd brought over the day before in lieu of payment. "I like being safe, and I'm not ashamed to admit it," she said, watching him go and stand at the window and look out at Lilly, who was having breakfast with a couple of sleepover friends in the fenced-in play yard.

Alain was an amazing man, really. Totally at

home wherever he was, doing whatever he was doing. Last night he'd held a sleepover for Lilly and invited a couple of the local girls, hoping they would help Lilly open up a little more. On her way in, she'd watched the girls interacting, and in a lot of ways Lilly reminded her of herself—the one always standing off to the side, watching. "And as much as you want to figure out what's going on with Lilly, it may not happen for a long time, Alain. If ever."

"She's so isolated."

"But at least she's there, part of the activity, including herself in it and not completely withdrawing. Which is a good thing."

"Delivering newborns is easier. You may have to figure out some physical problems along the way, but that's easy compared to this."

"You could be right. Being the outcast is always so…difficult. And no matter how hard you try to fit in, something never works, something that keeps you ostracized."

"Is that the way you were, Maggie? The one always off on the side, watching?'

Maggie took a sip of her coffee and sighed. "I was more like that than any of my other sisters. They were always so outgoing and I was so reserved. Sometimes to the point of being backward. At least by my family's standards."

"And your parents noticed?"

"Of course they noticed, and they worried a lot." She pulled a biscuit from the plate and broke off the end, then popped it in her mouth. Once she'd finished swallowing, she continued, "They wanted to fix me, probably like most good parents would want to do for their children. So they took me to a child psychologist, who assured them I was just being me. But that wasn't enough because I was so different. So I was taken to another psychologist and another. In total I can't even tell you how many psychologists I saw, and my parents never got the diagnosis they wanted, one that told them there was something wrong with their little girl. Something they could fix."

"So what did they do?"

"In the end, they left me alone to be the wall-flower I wanted to be. I mean, what else could they do other than institutionalize me or commit me to a lifetime of psychoanalysis for something that wasn't a problem for me?"

"Was that ever a consideration?"

Maggie laughed. "No. They knew I wasn't mentally ill but, in truth, I think the reason they dragged me to all these psychologists was to make sure that they weren't being bad parents to me. After all, we didn't have a traditional household. My parents both worked long hours, we had, as they call them today, *au pairs*. Several of them, actually, since there were seven of us girls.

"But the thing is, we were never neglected by our parents. One or both were always there when we had a part in the school play or ran in a track meet. One or both tucked us in every night of our lives. And we made a point of having several family meals together each week. Had movie night, and game night, and popcorn night. My parents gave us their best, but with me I think I made them feel like their best wasn't good enough, so they were looking for help, looking for a solution.

"But all these years later, when I think about it, I think it wasn't about me so much as it was about them. They loved me, but it was difficult having a child so different from the rest of them."

"So you think it's okay that Lilly's off standing under the oak tree while Sandra and Aureille are having a good time playing with their dolls?"

"I think it's a choice that Lilly's okay with, otherwise I think she'd be playing, too. And you do have to let her make some of her own choices, Alain. Or you're telling her that what she wants doesn't matter, which is pretty much where she is right now, believing that nothing about her matters."

He sighed the sigh of a troubled man. "But with her past…"

"Those are issues that will eventually have to work themselves out, but not until she's ready."

"Which will be when?" Alain asked as he watched Lilly move even farther away from the girls.

"Tomorrow or next year or never. Give her space, Alain. Which, by the way, is the same thing as respect. When she totally trusts you, if she's ready, she'll open up. Or not. It may not be in her nature to want to confide to anyone. But, in the meantime, at the risk of sounding like someone who's about to ask another some-one out on a date, how about dinner and a movie tonight? I have Leonie this evening, there's a good children's movie playing at the theater and I thought pizza would be the perfect food to go with the rest of it."

"Can I have popcorn?" he asked, smiling.

"With butter, if you behave."

"Behaving is underrated, but for butter on my popcorn…"

"Oh, and it's my treat."

It was like the room suddenly went cold. "You don't think I can spring for pizza and a movie?"

"Personally, I don't think you can spring for anything that isn't a necessity," she said. "And it wasn't meant to offend you. I just thought a nice evening out with the girls..."

"Charity date," he grumbled. "No, thanks. If I want pizza and a movie for Lilly, I'll pay for it."

Rather than being offended by his change in demeanor, Maggie merely laughed. "Male pride isn't very becoming on you, Alain. And it's going to deprive Lilly of a good time. Do you really want to be that selfish?"

"I can see why you were a loner. You were totally disagreeable, and even rude."

"Well, rude buys the pizza. Come by the house at six, and if you're still in a grumpy mood, drop off Lilly and go grumble in the swamp somewhere while the girls have a nice evening out. Oh, and if it makes you feel any better, we'll split the check. You pay for your pizza and popcorn, and I'll take care of me and the girls."

"Do you know how ridiculous that's going to look?"

"About as ridiculous as you sound," she quipped, then grabbed her white coat off the peg by the door and went to greet their first patient of the day, Minerva Jane Craig, who always refused to schedule an appointment. She was a bit of a drinker—homemade stuff—and couldn't understand the headaches that came in the morning. It was up to Alain and Maggie to sort headache from hangover.

As it turned out, pizza was good. Lilly ate with a voracity Alain hadn't seen in her yet. But the movie was another thing altogether, and it scared her to death. So much so that he cut his part of the evening short and left, carrying a very shaky little girl in his arms. Picture too large, noise too loud. Sensory overload, he supposed.

They spent the night at his house in town, a very uneventful night where they watched a little television, he popped corn she refused to eat and they both went to bed early. But in the middle of the night he got a call from Maggie, who'd gotten a call from Justin Bergeron who was on duty at the hospital, who'd gotten a call from his wife, Mellette, who'd gotten a call from Napoleon Dempsey who ran the Big Swamp gas station, and it seemed that Yasbeau Bonchance had come down sick and was close to being delirious, she was in such a bad way.

By the time Alain had cleared his head enough to pull on a pair of pants and a shirt, Maggie was at his front door, followed by her father, who had every intention of taking Lilly back to his home for the night.

"You're driving?" Alain asked.

"I'm faster than you. Know the roads better."

He couldn't argue with that. While he hadn't actually gotten lost out there, he had spent more time than he cared to admit winding the twisted roads—wrong twisted roads that lengthened his journeys. "So who is she and what are her symptoms?"

"I've never seen her before," Maggie said, phoning her sister. "Tell me about her," she said, then two minutes later related the description from Mellette. "She's in her mid-thirties, large, healthy in that she didn't ever come to see Eula as far as Mellette could remember. She's nice."

"So do we know what's wrong with her?" he asked, as Maggie took a turn in the road much faster than he would have and he ended up hanging on to the truck's door handle for dear life.

"Justin said she had a powerful hurt in her side."

"Right side?"

"He didn't say."

"So we could be looking at appendicitis. Or a ruptured cyst. Might be a gallbladder attack, depending where, on her side, the pain is located."

"Don't you ever get patients who aren't very communicative about their symptoms?" she asked him.

"Usually, by the time they get to me they're way more communicative than they need to be because they're scared to death. Seeing an obstetrician who deals with high-risk pregnancy for a problem is almost admitting to something you don't want to face—that there could be a problem with your pregnancy."

"I understand that maybe now more with Mellette than I did before, but still…" She shrugged and smiled as she rounded a gravel curve a little too fast, which threw Alain halfway across the seat until the seat belt locked down tight on him. "People will be people, I suppose. No changing human nature once it's set in."

"How about changing their driving style?" he choked out, unsnapping the belt to free himself and immediately snapping himself back into place.

Maggie laughed. "Sorry about that. One of the warnings about being the introverted girl was that when I turned sixteen and started to drive, I was hell on wheels. Guess having a big hunk of metal surrounding me made me feel brave or something."

"I think it left a bruise," he commented drily.

Maggie laughed again. "Want me to ice it up for you once we get there?"

"I want you to let me drive…always! Whenever we're in a car together, I drive."

"Talk like that could hurt my feelings," she said, teasing him as she slowed down for the next curve.

"Talk like that could save my life," he countered. "You don't drive like that with Mellette's daughter in your car, do you?"

"Actually, Mellette doesn't let me drive Leonie anywhere. That's why my dad always tags along. He's my designated driver."

"Instead of all that money they spent on shrinks for you, they should have saved it for a good driving instructor."

"You're blunt," she said as they pulled off the road onto a long, narrow lane that looked more like a pathway than a road.

"And you're not?" he countered, flinching

involuntarily as various vines and branches snapped against the car.

"I would never take one of your psychological vulnerabilities, like you're a baby when it comes to riding with someone else, and use it against you."

She was really enjoying this, enjoying the teasing and the light banter between them. Enjoying it almost as much as he was, and he couldn't, for the life of him, figure out someone as engaging as Maggie could have ever been such an introverted child. "And I would never blatantly tell you you're a menace on the road, except that's a fact of which I'm sure you're already aware."

"I've never been in a wreck," she said defensively, as the house where Yasbeau Bonchance lived with her husband, Henry, came into view.

"The day is just beginning," Alain said as he climbed out of the passenger's seat and grabbed his medical bag.

Yasbeau, as it turned out, was a very large woman, with a sweet smile. She offered to make coffee even though she was definitely in some pain. And her husband, Henry, who was equally as large, brought out a plate of leftover fried chicken in case anyone was hungry. At three in the morning, the snack, while appreciated, wasn't exactly what either Alain or Maggie wanted.

"When did this pain start?" Alain asked Yasbeau as Maggie started taking vital signs—temperature, pulse, blood pressure.

"Yesterday afternoon, when I was fixing Henry's lunch. He likes a big meal midday, since he does such hard work...he's a mechanic. So I cooked him up some black-eyed peas with fatback, corn bread and a bowl of greens. The pain came on when I was greasing up the skillet for the corn bread. It wasn't much, just a twinge, and I didn't think much about it. But it kept coming back, off and on through the day, and got powerful bad when I was frying chicken for Henry's dinner. That's when I had to go sit down for a while and wait for it to pass."

"And did it?" Alain asked.

"Some. It got lighter for a while. But I wasn't much hungry, so I didn't eat much. Henry, bless his heart, did the dishes for me while I settled in and watched some television. I must have dozed off, and Henry just put a blanket over me and let me sleep in my chair. Then a couple of hours ago I awoke with a powerful hurt, and it's not going away. In fact, it's getting worse."

"Where?" Alain asked as he took out the stethoscope and listened to Yasbeau's chest.

"Vitals all elevated," Maggie said.

Alain nodded, as Yasbeau indicated right-sided pain just below her rib cage. Then also indicated some behind her right shoulder blade.

"Any nausea or vomiting, or unusual belching?" he asked.

"Got me a terrible case of nausea," she said, "but not the other."

Alain moved his stethoscope down to Yasbeau's belly and asked her to please lift her blouse, which she did, but only after a stiff nod from her husband. As she was in the process of shifting around, another one of her spells hit and she almost doubled over with pain.

"It's getting worse, Doc," Henry said. "And it's taking her longer to get over each one."

"Gallbladder?" Maggie asked. "Pain's certainly in the right area."

"Maybe, but…" Alain held up his hand to quiet everybody in the room, then placed his stethoscope on Yasbeau's belly and listened for a second. After which he indicated for Maggie to hand him his bag, from which he pulled a different stethoscope. Maggie gasped and immediately turned and ran down the hall toward the bathroom to gather up an armload of clean towels, while Alain listened to a distinct heartbeat in Yasbeau's belly. Two, in fact.

Straightening back up, he looked at her, and she was as white as a ghost. "Have you ever had a baby?" he asked her.

She shook her head. "Henry and I've been married since I was fifteen and we haven't had the good fortune. So somewhere along the way we decided the good Lord didn't mean for it to happen for us."

"Have you had a period lately?"

Yasbeau shrugged, shook her head. "Never been regular that way. Eula wanted to give me some herbs to help fix that, but I figured I'd be better off just the way I…" Another labor pain hit, following only a couple minutes behind the first one Alain had witnessed.

"Is she…?" Maggie asked, setting the pile of clean towels down on a table next to where Yasbeau was sitting.

"Unless I heard wrong, which could happen, it may be twins."

"Twin what?" Henry asked.

"Babies," Alain said. "You wife is in labor and she's about to give birth. It might be twins."

"Can't be," Yasbeau gasped. "I'm getting too old for that. My mamma quit her childbearing years when she was thirty-five, and I'm already thirty-six." Another pain gripped her.

"Problem is, I have no way of knowing how far along these babies are," Alain said. "And since she obviously doesn't have a clue…"

"Dear God," Maggie said, pulling out her cell phone. "I don't know what kind of emergency transport we can get out here. If any…"

"Labor's fast," Alain said, standing up. "Yasbeau, I need to get you into your bed and take a look to see how this birth is progressing."

"Ain't no man ever looked down there," Henry piped up.

Alain smiled at him. "I deliver babies every day, and there's a good chance I might be delivering two here in the next hour or so. What I need you to do, Henry, to help your wife get ready for this is to boil me some water, and get me as many fresh sheets as you can find. I'll also need two boxes big enough to hold the babies, and I'll need the sheets in those boxes ready for the babies to stay warm in. Do you understand?"

Henry nodded, then a smile crossed his face. "I did twins?"

"Don't know for sure, but you may have. Oh, and, Henry, since Yasbeau hasn't had any doctor's care while she was pregnant, this may be a little rough. When it comes time for her to deliver, I need you to stand behind her and push her back up and hold her in a sitting position. She may be screaming, but can you do that for me?"

"I can," he said in all seriousness.

"Good. Now, get that water going, and find those boxes and sheets."

"Water?" Maggie asked.

"Need something sterile if I have to do a C-section."

"Oh, no! I hadn't even thought about that possibility."

Alain shrugged. "Trust me, it's a possibility."

Maggie made her phone calls while Alain helped Yasbeau into the bedroom, and by the time Maggie had managed to find an ambulance that would meet them halfway, Alain had Yasbeau ready to examine. It took him about one minute to shout, "These babies aren't waiting. One of them's crowning right now."

Maggie looked in over his shoulder and saw the top of the first baby's head. It was covered in a mass of black curls. Curls that were popping into the world at a rapid speed. "What can I do?" she asked him.

"Take the baby, clean it up as best you can. I have some clamps in my bag so use one for the umbilicus, then get the baby warm."

"Nothing like doing it the old-fashioned way," she said, as Alain helped maneuver the first baby into the world. A boy, fairly good-size, thank heavens. One who started thrashing and screaming the instant he had his first chance. "He looks good," she told Alain as he began his exam for the next baby.

"My kid?" Henry sputtered, with great emotion from his end of the bed.

"Your son," Maggie said, giving Henry a quick peek at the baby before prepping him and tucking him in to a sheet-lined box that had once cased canned green beans.

"Just the one?" Henry asked anxiously, as he held his wife's hand.

"Doctor is checking now to see if there's another one."

"And I'm sure there's one more on the way," Alain announced. "Just a little slower than the first one."

"We've got two," Henry announced pridefully to Yasbeau, as if she didn't already know.

"How far along?" Maggie asked Alain.

"I'm guessing somewhere close to thirty-four weeks," Alain said. "Breathing seems fine and everything looks normal, but I still want them to go in for a good checkup. Yasbeau, too, since she's done this thing without medical care."

"Go in, as in the hospital?" Henry asked.

"It's best for everyone."

"We don't like hospitals around here," Henry argued. "And my wife and children will be fine without them."

"They probably will," Alain argued back, "but do you want to take that kind of a risk? If everything goes well, they'll be in and out in a day or two."

"I think we should," Yasbeau said as the next labor pain struck. It had been fifteen minutes since the first baby, and a quick check showed that the second one was on its way, in a big hurry just like its big brother.

Ten minutes later, another fine little boy pushed its way into the world, and seemed as healthy as the first one, who'd already been named Henry John Bonchance, Junior. The second was tagged with John Henry Bonchance. Thankfully, there were no more babies to come.

"So what do we do about getting them to the hospital?" Maggie asked as she helped get Yasbeau cleaned up and ready for the trip while Alain examined the twins.

"One of us will have to take the babies to meet the ambulance, and one will take Yasbeau and

Henry. And I'm telling you right now, I'm driving the babies."

"You don't trust me?"

"I don't trust you so much that I've already asked Henry to drive his truck so you can look after his wife."

"I should get angry over that," Maggie said, "but I won't. It was an amazing night." Said as the sun was beginning to wake up over the swamp. "It's been a long time since I've assisted in anything like that and it kind of makes me miss nursing. Makes me wonder if I can squeeze in a few more hours at the clinic, or even at New Hope."

Alain smiled. It had been a good night. Two healthy twins had come into the world to a mother who hadn't even expected them but who was already proving she was going to be the best mother in the world. And he and Maggie had worked so well together. Yes, a good night all the way around, he decided as he handed off the babies and mom to the waiting paramedics at Dempsey's Gas Station a little while later.

Times like this made him want to get back into his kind of medicine so badly he could feel the physical ache of it. But there was also something else bothering him, something that would never be allowed. He'd enjoyed Maggie. Enjoyed her too much. Could even see the two of them, well… No point in thinking about that. She'd made herself perfectly clear on the subject, and Maggie didn't strike him as the kind of woman who'd change her mind once it was set.

Too bad. Because he could almost see great things with them.

CHAPTER SEVEN

"NOT BAD FOR a night's work," Maggie said, kicking off her shoes, pulling her feet up under her on the porch rocker and making herself comfortable in the throw pillows. They were sipping iced sweet tea and eating leftover sweet biscuits.

"Not bad for someone going in expecting appendicitis or worse and ending up with babies. It's been a long time since I've done any of the other procedures and trust me when I say I'd rather deliver twins any day of the week."

"Those babies were over five pounds each, and she never knew she was pregnant. How does something like that happen? How can a woman make it to almost full term and not even suspect she's pregnant?"

"Not enough education, for starters. People here, especially the women, could use some prenatal classes. Also, she didn't go to doctors, which didn't help matters any. That, plus she's a large woman. Some women close to menopause age never suspect that the end of their periods could signal a pregnancy and not the end of child-bearing days. My own mother thought she was in menopause and didn't even suspect pregnancy until she was well over six months along.

"So what happened isn't unheard of. In fact, it's more common than most people know. In fact, cryptic pregnancies—that's what they're called—happen where one woman in four hundred and fifty doesn't know they're pregnant until week twenty or later, and one in twenty-five hundred never know it until birth."

"Well, it scares the bejeebies out of me. So many things could go wrong, especially carrying twins. And she delivered less than a month early. Without complications. And the babies are perfect."

"As they say, ignorance is bliss. But she was a

healthy woman to begin with. Strong. Ate good foods, even though she's large. Didn't drink. Exercised. Had everything going for her that a doctor would prescribe. As a result, mom can come home today, and the babies will probably be home inside the week."

Maggie stretched back and looked up at the early sky. "How would it be to get up one morning without any knowledge that you're going to have a baby, then end up being a mother by the end of that day?" She took a sip of tea, then looked out over the yard at the lush greenery. The more time she spent in Big Swamp, the more it was growing on her. She liked the nature here. Especially liked the people.

In fact, she could almost see herself giving up the creature comforts she'd come to expect just to live in a place like this. How would it be to come home after work, spend her evenings and nights working in virtual solitude? No one interrupting her, no one expecting anything of her.

Where she lived, her condo was surrounded

by people, and shops, and blaring horns. People whizzed by all hours of the day on bicycles and scooters. Tour buses that made regular routes to the cemeteries, the Garden district and Jackson Square also slowed down so eager tourists could look at the front of the building where her condo was located.

See, what she hadn't learned until after she'd bought her condo was that the building was actually designated as haunted, making it one of the frequent stops on both bus and walking tours filled with people wanting to experience, first-hand, a real live ghost. Amazingly, on Fridays and Saturdays, she even had walking tours that came by at midnight, of all things!

So the solitude out here in Big Swamp was nice. Relaxing. Something she envied. Only thing was, the internet reception was spotty, and cell phone reception came and went, and she needed those connections to the outside world for her work. And the most convenient way in was by boat, right straight through the swamp, which she wasn't fond of. Still, it was a pleasant, if impractical, daydream.

"Actually, that did happen to me just recently. I woke up one morning all free and clear then ended up with a six-year-old child. For sure, it's a life-changer."

"But you're not going to keep her permanently, and that's the difference. There'll come a time when a nice foster or adoptive family will take her, and you'll be able to go back to being free and clear."

"Except children her age are hard to place. I talked to her social worker yesterday and, so far, no luck. No interest in anything, even temporary, and there's a long list of children younger than her waiting to be placed."

"But her placement eventually is something you're going to have to brace yourself for, Alain. Lilly is not your ready-made family and she won't be staying here. I know it's hard not to get attached to her, but on the other hand you could wake up any day and have her taken away from you, and that's just something you've got to be prepared to deal with. Just because she's hard to place right now doesn't mean she won't be placed."

"I'm aware of that, and I'm also aware that would be best for her," he defended himself. "And I want what's best for her, whether or not you think that."

"Oh, I think that. But your given choice in careers is delivering babies, so you must love them, maybe have a stronger bond than most people do because of your career choice, and it scares me to death that you're going to get too attached, then get hurt."

"I know what I'm dealing with here, Maggie. Professionally, emotionally…I go through this every day and know the end results. I don't keep the kids I deliver, and I don't expect to. But I do everything humanly possible to help them while they're under my care. That's what my life is about."

"But the babies you deliver aren't six, and in so much need."

He blew out an impatient breath. "I can draw the line."

"Can you?" she challenged.

"Why do you even care?"

"Because I like you, and I don't want to see you get hurt."

"I suffer through."

"Maybe you do, maybe you just keep it all in. Whatever the case, I'm betting that all that time in Afghanistan was difficult, seeing all those children in need and not able to do a thing to help them."

"That's a different story."

"Is it, Alain?"

"Okay, so maybe you don't get used to what you see going on around you every day, and you try to harden your heart to it. But there's so much of it, and when I was…injured…and I was in the hospital, recovering at first then doing light duty for several weeks, I was in the same hospital where they were taking civilian casualties and it was…tough. I'll admit it. But working in the orphanage, then being there, that didn't make me want to take every single one of them under my wing, so to speak. It just made me glad that in some ways I'd been able to help."

"But Lilly reminds you of one of those children, and it's become personal. She's the one you can do more for than just help. And even if you don't know that intellectually, you feel it emotionally."

"Or you're completely wrong. Maybe I'm just being a doctor who cares for his patient, and Lilly's a patient with extraordinary needs."

"Maybe." Maggie nodded, but she wasn't sure his heart was in his defense. Alain Lalonde was a hard person to get to know, and while on the exterior he just didn't seem the type who wanted that kind of intense emotional involvement with a child, on the inside was he as different as he claimed to be? She did question that. More than that, she was attracted to the part of him he denied. Pretty package to look at, but even prettier down deep. Except she didn't do the down-deep part herself. It was too risky, and more than anyone she knew, she knew exactly who she was and what she wanted.

Also, she was very unbendable about those things. Not even when it came to Alain, a man she was finding herself extremely attracted to. "You may understand all that intellectually, but it's still difficult having people ripped out of your life, especially once they've found a place in your heart."

"The heart heals."

"Does it?"

"Something bad happens, a heart breaks, but people move on with their lives."

"They move on, changed. Because the heart doesn't heal so much as it bends to accept whatever happens." She shook her head. "And while the heart may have this amazing ability to stretch itself in new directions, I don't think it ever really heals from being broken. My sister, after her first husband died, found a new love, but that doesn't mean her heart isn't still broken over her first love. It's just…"

"Reshaped?"

"Reshaped," she agreed.

"Then what you're telling me is that your heart could reshape, too, to where it includes wanting a different life. Maybe a home and family."

"I…I don't think so. That's a whole different argument."

"Is it?"

"Of course it is. We were talking about broken hearts, not reshaping a life."

"Well, for whatever it's worth, I think you'd be a sensational wife and mother, and I don't think there needs to be that much reshaping."

"A sensational mother who would be more devoted to her work than her child. That's not a good definition of sensational, Alain. That's more a definition of someone who'd suck at it. Look, I've got a legal client to see at noon, and a full afternoon of research ahead of me. Then tomorrow I've got to go into court with Jean-Pierre in the morning, and I've got promised hours at the hospital on the evening shift.

"Most likely I'm not going to make it back out here to help you for at least two days, maybe more than that, depending on how my casework goes. Will you be okay on your own? Because if you think you'll need help, I'm pretty sure Daddy would love to come out and put on his stethoscope."

"I think I'll be fine."

"But with taking care of Lilly? Are you sure?"

He smiled. "Where there's a will, there's a way. And that goes for everything in life."

"Unless your will gets stretched too thin."

"Like yours does sometimes?"

"That's not a nice thing to say. I manage to manage quite well, thank you very much." She was actually offended that he thought she tended to overdo things. If nothing else, she'd shown him how utterly efficient she was in everything she did. Maybe even went out of her way just a little to prove it to him.

"Look in the mirror, Maggie. You're a beautiful woman, but you don't smile much, and you look just plain tired. And you can't deny it because you can't be objective."

"Nothing a good night's sleep won't fix."

"If you allow yourself that good night's sleep. Which you won't."

She squared indignant shoulders. "Why do you even care?"

"Because you work for my defense attorney, and I need my team fresh and eager, not tired and cranky."

"You're being serious, aren't you?" she asked him.

"Dead serious. You push yourself past the point of common physical sense and you, with your medical background, should know better than most people."

Part of what he was saying was right. She did push herself. Got by on too little sleep and too much caffeine. But that wouldn't last forever. Thirty-four weeks, count them. Thirty-four weeks and she'd graduate from law school. Then she could cut that activity out of her life and move on into something better. It was a plan... her plan. And the end was finally in sight. "What I know is that you don't have the right to interfere."

"Maybe I interfere because I care."

"Well, don't. It won't get you anywhere." That was the truth, plain and clear.

True to her word, Maggie was nowhere to be seen for three days, which left Alain plenty of time to be doctor, carpenter and even father. He and Lilly were falling into a routine, though. They'd have breakfast in the morning, after which he'd spend a couple hours homeschooling her. Apparently Lilly had had no formal or informal training whatsoever. She couldn't read or do the simplest math, let alone do any rudimentary writing or printing, but she was an eager, smart learner, and he'd have been willing to bet that she'd catch up to children her own age in no time at all.

After homeschooling, he either worked as a doctor, if he had patients to see, which was becoming more and more the case. Then Lilly would play in her play yard, looked after by one of the local ladies who'd volunteered to help. More like, she held back and simply watched what went on around her. Then Alain would take a quick lunch break with Lilly, after which he went back to work. But as he doctored he supervised the building crews, who were getting closer to finishing the surgery.

Then in the evening he'd spend another couple of hours homeschooling Lilly, they'd have dinner together, she'd refuse to play games but she would settle into watching television occasionally. Then off to bed. Lilly first, then himself a couple of hours later, after he'd read some articles in various medical journals.

And with each passing day he was becoming

more and more frustrated that he couldn't draw Lilly out of her shell. "Be patient with her," the social worker had said. But it wasn't Lilly he was losing patience with. It was himself, for not finding a way to get through to her. Which made him feel like a failure more and more.

"She's come up in uncertainty," Amos Picou said one evening as he stopped by for coffee, and to bring by a batch of herbs he'd picked fresh that day. "And that's all she knows."

"What she knows is that she doesn't trust me," Alain snapped.

"You're right about that. That child doesn't know how to trust anybody, and how can you blame her, coming from where she did, always getting yelled at no matter what she did?"

"I don't even want to think about where she came from," Alain said. "It's depressing, and so damned frustrating not to be able to change the way she was raised. Makes me want to go hit something or someone."

"Ah, but there's where you go wrong. You have

to think about where she came from, and what happened to her there, which will help you understand what scares her so much. They're tied together, Doc. Part of who she is, part of who she'll always be."

"Then you don't think she can overcome her past."

Amos laughed. "No, we can never overcome it, and maybe we shouldn't because it's what makes us who we are, gives us the strength to get along in this world. But we can get past it. We all do, if we're strong enough and want it badly enough. Although I think some folks like using it as an excuse. But not Lilly. I see real strength and determination in that child."

"But how do you help someone get past it? I guess that's the question I have. How can you help someone get past something that's changed their life?"

"You wouldn't be talking about Lilly now, would you?"

"It's that obvious?"

"You get that moony look every time Maggie comes around. Anyone with any sense can see it."

"Except the one who's supposed to see it."

"She's just set in her ways. Knew me a gal like that once. Stubborn. Dear heavens, she had a stubborn streak in her that wouldn't have budged for anything. And I obliged that in her because I was always too afraid that if I did anything else she'd send me packing. Miss Eula Bergeron..."

"As in Eula's House?"

Amos nodded. "The sun rose and set in her as far as I was concerned, but I never took the chance to tell her because having her on her terms was better than not having her at all. When I was younger I should have done something about it. Should have taken that woman in my arms and told her how I felt and accepted the consequences one way or another, but I didn't. Then time passed and we got stuck in our routines."

"You never knew if she reciprocated your feelings?"

"Never knew. Never will. And that's the worst part. If I'd known, I could have done something about it. Maybe fought harder to win her hand if she wasn't in the mood to get caught, marry her if that's something she had had a mind to do, or get on with another life altogether. But my choice was to stay here, look after my herbs and be her friend. It was good, but it was never enough. And I've got to tell you, son. You've got one a lot like Eula. But if you want my advice, you'll be smarter than I was."

"She doesn't want a traditional domestic kind of life. No entanglements—husband, kids or otherwise."

"Then you intending on keeping Lilly?"

"Haven't given it a lot of thought yet, but I might. We seem to work out well together, and she does need consistency."

"Boy, you sure got some learning to catch up on. Consistency is never any reason to adopt a child…or go after a woman. You'd best get to thinkin' hard on your real feelings before it's too late, because if you think the adoption board's going to give you that child because you have a consistent relationship, you're in for a rude awakening. And I hope to God that word never comes into play between you and Maggie or you'll end up like me, picking herbs in the swamp all alone and swapping stories with neighbors."

Amos stood. "I've got a good gumbo on the stove and some corn bread just waiting to be cooked. Call Maggie, and I'll see the three of you around seven. Oh, and I'd be obliged if you'd tell Maggie to let her sister know I'll be sending a pot of leftovers her way. Mellette and Justin love my cooking. I'd like to think it's one of the things that got them together. That, and a relationship that wasn't based on consistency."

"I didn't say Maggie and I had a relationship based on consistency."

"Didn't have to say it, boy. It's written all over you." Laughing as he walked away, he called out,

"'Consistent man looking for consistent woman for a consistent relationship.' Now, that's a lonely heart ad that'll have 'em lining up at your door."

Alain's response was to pick up a piece of pea gravel and throw it at the man. It landed about a foot away from Amos's boot, and Amos just laughed as he continued to amble on. "Not very consistent with your throwing aim either, are you, boy?"

"It's not a date," Alain told himself as he looked in the mirror to make sure he looked presentable for an evening of gumbo at Amos Picou's. A plaid cotton shirt, jeans, boots—nice but not overdressed. The event had grown to include Maggie's parents, a couple of her sisters and even Justin was going to bring Mellette out for the evening because she was going stir-crazy, staying all cooped up and in bed much of the time. A few of the locals were stopping by, as well. Everybody bringing food. In other words, party!

Yet it felt like a date to Alain, probably because Amos had called a while ago and told him his date for the evening had accepted the invitation.

"Will there be lots of people there?" Lilly asked as she shied into the corner of the bedroom.

"Maggie and her family will be there. You remember Leonie, and she'll be there. And a few friends from Big Swamp will be stopping by, as well."

"Don't want to go," Lilly said, big tears welling in her eyes.

This was, perhaps, the first time Lilly had expressed an opinion, and it surprised him. "Why not?" he asked her. "Everybody there will be very nice."

"*They* might be…"

"Be what?"

"Stealing things from people who go to parties, when they left their houses to go." She was referring to her aunt and uncle. "They would make me sneak in and take things like money and pretty things on shelves, and sometimes if I got caught or took the wrong things they'd..."

"What, sweetheart?" he asked gently.

"They'd lock me in the closet, or make me stay outside all night, all by myself."

Dear God, what she must have suffered. "But they won't be there at the party. And what if I promise to hold your hand and never let go of it?"

Lilly shook her head adamantly. "They'll come and look in the windows to see who's there, so they can go steal from them. They always do and no one sees them. If they see me there, or you..."

"Are you afraid they'll come here, too?" he asked, wondering if she also lived in that sort of terror. "To this house?"

Lilly nodded. "If we go to the party."

"Then we won't go," he said, even though he was disappointed to miss the evening, and the chance to spend time with Maggie. But none of that mattered. Lilly was terrified of being in crowds and he wasn't about to put her through any more hell than she'd already experienced. "In fact, how about we go to town and have pizza?"

That brought a wan smile to her face.

"Then there's this place we could go get ice cream."

"Can Maggie come, too?"

"She's going to be spending the evening with Amos Picou and his guests so, no, not this time. But you like her?"

"She would be like my mommy, if I had one. Someone who was nice, and never yelled."

"Was your mommy like that?"

Lilly nodded. "She made me nice clothes, and sometimes, when she could, she bought me toys."

Yet left her child to people like the Aucoins. Of course, Lilly's mother might not have known. Or there might have been extenuating circumstances that forced such a choice. But, still, to leave your child to people like that? It made him shudder, just thinking about it. "Well, when I call Amos and tell him we won't be there, I'll let Maggie know you'll miss her tonight. Will that be okay?"

"Thank you," Lilly said shyly.

Several minutes later, after he'd made his apologies to Amos, he found himself on the phone with Maggie, explaining the situation. "Oh, and just so you know, Lilly said if she had a mother she'd be just like you. That's in case you want to dispel the myth that you're not parenting material."

"A mommy like me? Are you sure that's what she said?"

"Exact words. Because you're nice. She thinks you'd make her pretty clothes."

"Except I can't sew, I can't cook and I don't know how to relate to a child for more than a couple of hours. Great mother material that is."

"Well, you may have yourself convinced one way, but Lilly is certainly convinced another."

"We all do that, don't we? See what we want

to see. Anyway, sorry you can't make it. Amos makes the best gumbo in these parts and this is turning into quite the party."

He was sorry, too, but about more than just the gumbo. "Well, be on the lookout for Lilly's aunt and uncle peeking in the windows, because that's the kind of event they like to stake out." Except for this once, they wouldn't have Lilly to do it for them. Would that throw them off their game? Or did it really matter?

As he took her hand and led her to the truck, he wondered about a lot of things. About Lilly, first and foremost. And about Maggie. Then somewhere in there he did let the thought enter that he might just like to keep Lilly, adopt her and raise her the way she needed to be raised. But he feared that would preclude Maggie from ever being more than she was to him, and one of those thoughts went far beyond friendship.

It was an impossible situation. No matter how it worked out, he couldn't have it every way he wanted. But he sure didn't like the idea of picking and choosing, either.

"Pepperoni?" Lilly asked when she climbed in the truck.

"Extra pepperoni." No, he sure didn't like the idea of picking and choosing. Wasn't sure he could. Or how he would, if it came right down to it.

CHAPTER EIGHT

"LOOKS LIKE YOU two are having all the fun, and I'm missing out." Maggie sat down at the extra chair at the table and signaled the server over. "Mind if I join you?" she asked Alain. "Or is this a private party?"

Lilly's face lit up. "I wanted you to come with us. He didn't," she said, pointing a serious and accusatory finger at Alain. "He said you had other things to do."

Alain chuckled. "It's not that I didn't want you to have pizza with us. But I did explain your previous engagement with Amos Picou to Lilly and told her that's where you'd be this evening, having dinner there with those friends and family."

"An extra plate and an iced tea," she said to the server, who scurried right away. "Well, that's where I started my evening, but this sounded like more fun. So if you don't mind sharing your pizza with me, I'd love to stay." She smiled. "Besides, as much as I love a good gumbo, and I must admit that I had a taste of Amos's and it was heaven, I do like a good pizza just as much." She turned to Lilly. "Especially the pepperoni."

"Pepperoni gumbo?" Lilly asked innocently. "Maybe you should tell Amos his gumbo needs lots of pepperoni."

"And maybe I will next time I see him."

"Well, as you can see, we have plenty to share." Almost two-thirds of the entire pie was still uneaten, still warm and, oh, so inviting so she dug right in. "So why are you here with us, Maggie, when Amos was throwing the party of the season?"

"Too many people. Too much noise. I was already tired, and by the time I left, half of Big Swamp had dropped in, bringing their own gumbos, etoufees, jambalayas, okra casseroles, bodin sausages, dirty rice, crawfish pies… It was overwhelming and yummy, but the walls were closing in. I'm not so…"

"Social?" he asked.

"I'm social, but in smaller proportions. Especially when I've had a long, long day. And people were just falling all over each other there were so many of them, so I was glad when Amos made your excuses because that gave me my own excuse to crawl out the door and sneak away. So why didn't the two of you go over there?"

"Pretty much the same reason. Lilly's not fond of large crowds, and I can take them or leave them," he said, dishing up another piece of pizza. "Well, it sounds to me like a brilliant idea, coming here."

"Can I go play in the balls?" Lilly asked shyly. She was referring to a large castle-like blown-up contraption filled with soft balls, designed to let children play and bounce in it. "I'm done with my pizza."

"Think they'll let me play in the balls, too?" Alain asked.

"No, silly. You're too big."

"Then I guess you can go play, but I'll be watching."

With that, Lilly scampered off to join three or four other children in the balls.

"So what's the story?" Maggie asked.

"Her aunt and uncle are sneak thieves who have a habit of robbing people's houses when they attend parties. Apparently they put her to work at it as well, and Lilly was afraid they'd be at Amos's party, looking in the window to see who was there and see me, then go and rob the clinic. So she didn't want to go."

"You're a good temporary dad, bringing her here," she said, reaching across the table to squeeze his hand. But the squeeze turned into more of a hand hold, where their fingers entwined, then lingered that way much longer than either of them had intended.

"It's not so bad when you're being daddy to someone like Lilly. She's easy to care for."

"Have you ever thought of having children of your own?" Maggie asked him.

"Not really. It takes two, and I've never found my other half. I suppose when I do, a family won't be out of the question. And you?"

"I don't have time. I've made choices that..." She looked down at their entwined fingers and pulled her hand away. "That wouldn't leave me time to be a mother."

"Conscious decision?"

"Not that so much as the way it worked out. You know what they say about making your bed then having to lie in it."

"But you can always shake up the bed, can't you? Or buy a new one?"

"I like my old bed. It suits me. No shaking, and no new bed needed."

"To bad. You'd be a brilliant mother."

"Seriously? How do you figure that?"

"I see the way you look at Lilly, with...I guess you'd call it longing. And the way you love your niece. I think you underestimate yourself."

"Or you overestimate me."

"Hey, you're here with Lilly and me tonight, eating pizza, rather than being at Amos's, eating his world-famous gumbo. That says something."

"Maybe it does, but I'm not sure what." She sat back in her chair and fixed her attention on Lilly, who was having the time of her life jumping up and down in the blow-up castle filled with balls. If only life was that simple.

Ten minutes later, when Lilly had returned to the table, Alain suggested they leave and go for ice cream.

"Ice cream?" Lilly practically squealed.

"A little girl's dream night," Alain said.

"It would be her dream night if someone would allow me to buy her pink shoes, as well."

He smiled. "That from the nonmom type."

"I was a little girl once and I know how important these things are. So are we in for the shoes, as well?"

He looked across the table at Maggie and her eyes were shining almost as brightly as Lilly's, and for a second a lump caught in his throat when he thought of them as the perfect little family. They weren't, of course, and he knocked that notion out of his head almost as fast as it entered. This was temporary, he told himself as they finished up the pizza. It might last another few days, maybe a week or two, but then it would be over with. Over. Done. He'd be back to being on his own without the responsibility of one little girl. The thought of that didn't settle well with his pizza.

"If they're really that important…"

"Trust me," Maggie said. "They are. So do either of you know of a place where we can find some pretty pink shoes?"

"I do!" Lilly exclaimed as she took Maggie by the hand and led her in the complete opposite direction from which they'd come. "And they have sparkles on them. And purple stars."

"Oh, my," Maggie said as they passed the window of the shop for little girls' things. "Is that them?"

Lilly nodded. "They're beautiful, aren't they? Like the shoes a fairy princess would wear."

"Well, they look a little small for me, but maybe they might have a pair that would fit you."

"Really?" Lilly looked up at Alain. "Would it be okay to go see?"

Damn, his heart just swelled every time Lilly looked at him, especially with such wonderment. She was such an abused little girl, yet she was such a typical little girl in so many ways, and he was glad that Maggie had had the common sense to know that Lilly not only wanted these shoes, she needed them to help make her normal. Glad she not only knew but had banged it through his thick skull.

"It would be very okay," he said as he opened the door for his two ladies.

An hour later they emerged with shopping bags full of shoes and socks and clothes—nothing practical the way he would have picked them all. But everything was frivolous and feminine and every six-year-old girl's dream. "See, now, that's the way to go shopping," Maggie commented as they wandered on down the street, hand in hand in hand.

"My idea of shopping is get in, get what you need, get out as fast as you can," Alain replied. "Anything else is a waste of time."

"Typical man," Maggie snorted.

"Typical man," Lilly echoed, and they all laughed as they headed off for ice cream.

Maggie had really given this a tremendous amount of thought on the way over here this evening. Why had she wanted to come? What did it mean? Why, if she knew she didn't want to get involved, was she putting herself in the direct line of involvement? And nothing could have possibly been more direct than this.

Okay, so maybe she just liked the male companionship. It had been years since Marc and she was, after all, human, subject to the same frailties and foibles all humans were. So maybe she was simply in the mood for some male companionship, and Alain was safe owing to one little girl tagalong. Nowhere in her arguments did she simply make a case for wanting to see Alain on his own, without child. No, that had never entered the mix because Lilly made it safe for her.

But when she'd stepped into the pizza parlor and hidden near the door, simply watching them interact for five minutes, why had her heart knocked a little harder than it usually did? And why had her cheeks flushed a little more scarlet? Was it because she was afraid that was what she wanted deep down, and didn't even know it or recognize it or want to know it? Or was it because she was afraid she'd get entangled in it somehow when she knew she didn't want it?

So maybe she was choosing Alain because he was safe. Why not? There was safety in numbers, especially when one of those numbers came in the form of a child.

On one hand he would take care of a certain need in her for male companionship, which she did sorely miss. But on the other, he had Lilly, the ultimate safety net. Also, there was that little clause in her contract that wouldn't let her outright date him, either. Meaning she was playing it safe all the way around with a man she found attractive. Whatever that meant.

"By the way, I have an appointment in Illinois on Monday to interview the woman who's suing you," she said casually as they headed toward the ice-cream parlor and Lilly stopped at practically every shop to gaze in the window.

"That easily?"

"No, nothing's ever that easy. But her attorney is paying me the courtesy of a short interview, with the stipulation that you're not there. She doesn't want to face you, which is exactly why I think you should go with me."

"Why?"

"Mrs. Gaines, the woman suing you, has guilty feelings. In my experience, people with guilty feelings are hiding something. It took some convincing to get her agree to sit down with me informally, and I promised you wouldn't be in that meeting, but nothing says you can't be in the hall outside. Or I might just insist on having you in the room, anyway. Who knows?

"Anyway, they're willing to talk settlement now. I put it out there on the table, and it wasn't flat-out rejected, which makes me even more suspicious." She smiled. "I've got a couple more hunches to play out, but I think that by the time I get to the table with the opposition, we're going to be in a pretty good position."

"You're that optimistic?"

"I'm never *that* optimistic until I've played all my cards and come up with the best hand."

"Which you expect to have?"

"Which I hope to have, otherwise I wouldn't have called the meeting. Oh, and Lilly's not cleared to leave the state, so my dad will look after her for a couple of days."

Alain swallowed hard. "I don't know what I'd do without the Doucet family. It's like you've stepped into every facet of my life and made it better."

Maggie smiled. "We're like that. Once we take you in, we don't let go very easily."

The next thirty minutes in the ice-cream parlor turned out to be the best for Lilly, who never stopped giggling as she ploughed into her bowl of ice cream. Afterward, she proclaimed, "This was the best night I ever had," then smiled all the way back to the car, juggling her packages, wearing her pink shoes, with a belly full of chocolate with sprinkles.

To be honest, it was one of the best nights Alain had ever had as well, and he hated seeing it come to an end. But it was over sooner than he liked, and Lilly was asleep almost before she'd climbed into the car.

"I'm glad she had a good time," Maggie said.

"And I'm glad you came along. The pink shoes..."

She shook her head. "It wasn't about the pink shoes. I enjoyed the company. Being with the two of you this evening was nice, and while I don't usually relate so well to children, Lilly is an exception. She's very…mature. Fun to be around, like my niece is."

"Maybe you like children more than you think."

"It's not that I dislike children. It's what I said earlier about not seeing myself in the role of mother and protector on a daily basis. My sister Mellette is a natural, and she'd be happy with a dozen children. They complete her life.

"But for me…I don't know how to explain it other than I don't need a child to make me feel complete. I'm already a complete person and I don't have any burning desire to pile onto that." She looked into the backseat at Lilly, who was snoozing peacefully. "She's an amazing little girl who's got a lot ahead of her to face. Have you ever considered keeping her? Because I think you'd be a perfect father for her."

"Actually, I have given it some thought. Haven't come to any conclusions yet, but I do like having her around. She seems to fit into my life quite easily, like she's supposed to be there."

"Well, for what it's worth, I watched the two of you this evening, and you seem natural together. I think you make her feel safe because she comes out of her shell when the two of you are interacting. At times, it was like watching a little girl who adores her daddy."

"My only fear is that she's going to become too attached to me, then the court will place her with someone else. I mean, what's that going to do to her?"

"Don't let them place her with anyone else. Fight for her, Alain. I'm sure Jean-Pierre will be glad to handle the legal end of it. Two of his children are adopted, and he's very much an advocate for placing children in the right situation."

"Sounds like you're trying to push her on me."

Maggie smiled. "Maybe I am. Just a little. Anyway, it's time to get her home and tucked in. You're not going all the way back out to the swamp tonight, are you?"

"I think we'll go back to my place," Alain said.

"Lilly's too tired to take very far, and I'd like to get her settled into bed sooner rather than later."

"Mind if I come along and help tuck her in?" Maggie asked impulsively. "It's on my way home, and since its Friday night I don't mind avoiding the walking tours for a little while longer."

"Ah, ghosts." Alain laughed. "Hope your ghost is amiable."

"Can't say that I've ever had the pleasure of meeting him, but he must be somewhat amiable to put up with me and all my strange hours. Or maybe ghosts don't really have a connection to real time the way we do."

"Well, you're welcome to come back to my place where there's a definite connection to real time. I can't promise you ghosts and tourists, but I do have my share of scaffolding and paint buckets and furniture covered with sheets."

"You don't mind if I follow you home?"

He shook his head. "And I'm sure Lilly would

love to have you there for her bedtime story, if she's awake enough to hear one tonight."

"You read her bedtime stories?"

He nodded. "It just seemed like the right thing to do. And she enjoys them."

Maggie was touched by all the efforts Alain made to make Lilly comfortable in a world that had been pretty cruel to her. More than that, it was occurring to her that she, Maggie, was becoming more and more attracted to Alain, which didn't make sense because while he was everything she wanted in a man, he was also everything she didn't want. That, plus she'd actually encouraged him to adopt Lilly.

Maybe that was her out strategy, her way of making sure the attraction didn't go any further than attraction. Because his legal case would be over with one day, maybe even by Monday, then she'd have some real emotions to deal with. So build up the man she could want into the kind of man she didn't want…

It was too confusing. Too manipulative. Better

to just let it turn into whatever it was meant to be and deal with the consequences at the time. Besides, she'd made a pretty strong case against wanting the domestic life, and Alain certainly seemed like that was what he wanted. So she'd thrown out all the signals, and she was damned sure he'd read them. Meaning she was safe.

But she wasn't sure if being safe made her happy or sad.

Maggie followed Alain to his house, where Alain carried Lilly up his front stairs and through the front door. "No ghosts, but lots of activity. Or, at least, I've never encountered a ghost. Maybe there used to be one until I started all the banging and ripping out walls."

"Could be your ghost hooked up with my ghost and they've gone off to find someone better to haunt." Maggie pulled off Lilly's shoes and socks, then took the child from Alain's arms. "Which room?"

"We're staying downstairs, first one on the

right. Eventually it'll be the parlor, but for now it's set up to be her temporary bedroom."

"And where are you staying?" she asked, once they'd tucked Lilly into bed.

"Next door to her, in the dining room. Sleeping on a cot." He smiled. "Not exactly the best accommodation, but it beats sleeping on the bare wooden floor."

"It's a beautiful house, Alain. How did it become so…rundown?"

"My elderly aunts owned it and never really trusted caretakers to do any of the odd jobs a place like this requires. Then one of my aunts passed, and the other one just moved out and shut it up for nine years. Left it the way it was the day she walked out, including a stained porcelain teacup in the kitchen sink. Anyway, after all the legal proceedings against me started, and I was virtually penniless, she just gave me the house. Said it was my inheritance anyway, and that I could sell it or keep it and live in it, whatever suited me.

"And since this had been my great-great-grandparents' home, and also because I was basically homeless, I decided to fix it up then figure out what to do with it. But the more work I put into it, the more I'm inclined to want to stay here."

"I can't blame you. All the fixtures are original—gas converted to electric. And the trim work… It's like my parents' house in elegance, or could be like their house when it's completed, but I think it will be even nicer because it has a family history." She pulled back a dusty old sheet and looked at the gold silk settee underneath. "Original furniture, too? Real Victorian?"

"Everything's the way I always remember it being, and I suppose that would be Victorian. I'm betting you'll find some old Victorian clothes in the wooden chests in the attic. Something my great-great-grandmother might have worn. I know I used to play with the toys and clothes I found in those chests when I was a child, and it was like stepping back in time."

"Oh, my. And it just sat here empty all this time without being vandalized?"

"Maybe because it looked so rundown no one would have guessed what was inside. Or maybe because my family hooked up a modern alarm system to it even before my aunt moved out, and it's been monitored all these years, even though it was deserted."

Maggie brushed her fingers over the settee. "Once upon a time I pictured myself living in a place as amazing as this. I was quite a reader, did that rather than watch television and play. And I read about all these beautiful Southern mansions, and how life had been back in the 1800s when they were built. I used to fantasize about making a grand entrance down a staircase just like the one here, and being the belle of the ball."

"So what happened to the little girl with the big dreams?"

"She started reading her parents' medical texts and couldn't put them down. Got hooked on the more practical side of life. Pretty soon the belle of the ball wanted to be a nurse."

"Just as admirable," he said as he took one more look in at Lilly and shut her door all but a crack, then turned to face Maggie. "But did she ever go back to revisit her belle-of-the-ball days, even for just a few minutes, or did that dream just disappear?"

Maggie shook her head. "Her life got involved in other ways…ways she liked better. Ways that suited her better, too."

"So withdrawing from the ball was your idea?"

"Withdrawing from the ball seemed the more practical thing to do in my case. I had sisters who also wanted to be belles of their own balls, and it just seemed silly for me to have those kinds of dreams, especially since…"

"Since you were the practical sister in the family."

"Something like that. We all have to grow up some time, don't we? I just did my growing up a little early."

"Maybe, but didn't you deprive yourself of a childhood? Because you didn't even allow yourself to have any fun when you'd hit that stage where a young person is supposed to experiment to find out which way their life is supposed to take them. Is that what happened to you, Maggie? You purposely stalled yourself?"

"Not stalling, because I already knew where I was going."

"Something else could have been out there for you, if you'd looked."

"Except I was pleased with my choice. Got even more pleased when I found a way to merge my love of medicine to my love of the law. Both things are pure. They don't let you down."

"And you never, ever let down a little, just to have fun?" he asked as he stepped closer to her.

"Never. Not enough time."

"Because you don't want to make the time," he said, reaching out and stroking her cheek.

"Alain, we can't do this. It's in the contract..."

"You'll always find an excuse, won't you, Maggie?"

"But we have this legal agreement."

"And if we didn't, what would be your next excuse?"

"I don't need an excuse."

"Then let me tear up that contract so we can see what happens. No one can force me into honoring it, especially as it's all pro bono work."

"But it wouldn't be ethical," she argued, holding her ground, not backing away from him even a few inches.

"Not if you were to tell anybody, which you wouldn't. But what goes on between you and me privately…"

"Why are you doing this to me?" she asked. But there was no challenge in her voice. More like giving in.

"And why are you staying here, asking me, if you really weren't opposed to it? In fact, why did you come and have pizza with us, and spend the evening with us, and follow me home?"

"Because you're my client, and—"

"And your client is about to kiss you. Which is what you want, isn't it? Oh, and if you need a reason for what I'm about to do, one that would hold up in a court of law, it's because…"

"Because why?" she whispered as his lips dipped down dangerously close to hers. So close she was on the verge of melting into him completely.

"Because I want to," he said as his lips sought hers. "Even though I know you're doing your best to push me away from you, I still want to."

"I'm not pushing," she argued.

"Sure you are. You tell me how you don't want children, don't want to be involved in any form of domesticity, then plead your case for my adopting Lilly. Yet you stand here, wanting this kiss as much as I do. Knowing full well one kiss could turn into so much more."

"That's not true. I wasn't…"

He chuckled. "Sure you were. And I'm on to you, Magnolia Doucet. You're human. Have human needs and wants and desires just like the rest of us. And as you try to distance yourself from all that, you really don't want to be distanced. It an excuse that keeps you safe, though. Except nothing about us is safe, and you already know that. I was aware of it for a full week when you watched me from the porch while I was working and you were sipping lemonade with your sister. Watching me, Maggie. Watching *me*. Not the work, not the other shirtless men. But me!"

"You were a hard worker."

"And you're lying to yourself."

"There was nothing else to watch."

"You could have been reading one of your medical or law texts."

"I wasn't in the mood."

His lips dipped even closer. "Because you were in the mood for me. Admit it, Maggie."

"You looked good in…sweat." She swallowed hard. "Great in sweat." She shut her eyes, felt the sweat rising up between the two of them.

"But you're not what I want, Alain. We need to be practical about this. I don't want—"

"Just for once, let's concentrate on what you do want. And you do want this, don't you?"

"No, I…"

"Admit it, Maggie. You want it."

"No, I don't." His lips were so close to hers now, a hair couldn't have separated them.

"Give in to it, Maggie. Take what you want, not what your head dictates. Only your heart, Maggie. Only your heart."

"Yes, I…I…"

The kiss was light at first. More like a gentle brushing. Or tickling. But when she didn't resist it, he pushed harder, pried her lips apart with his tongue and delved in like a starving man. A man who hadn't had the taste of a woman on his tongue for decades or beyond.

Her response at first was almost a paralyzing shock. Even though she expected the kiss, maybe even wanted it in some way she didn't understand, she stiffened under it, didn't melt into him naturally. Didn't fit the curves of her body to his. In fact, she felt like a board she was so stiff and frightened, felt like she would break in two if he held her any tighter. Yet she didn't want to stop. And in an instant when he let up to catch his breath, her heart pounded hard against his chest and she thought that this would be the last of it, that Alain would come to his senses and end it.

But his breath was his second wind, and the next time he kissed her he ground himself hard into her, his body matching equally to hers, knocking out all her stiff reserve and demanding the truest melding of man and woman. Which she gave him. Weakly. Without breath. And with more passion than she'd ever known in herself.

"I… We…" she gasped, trying to pull back, but he wouldn't let her pull back, and she didn't fight him to get away. "We can't do this," she finally managed. "Really, we can't."

"I'd say we do it very well."

"My job… That really is an obstacle."

"Who's to know?" he said as he kissed his way around her neck, taking pleasure in her shivers.

"I'm to know."

"And will you report yourself?" he continued as his tongue grazed across her jaw and down her throat.

"No, but…" She wanted to shudder, to give in to the pure pleasure and forget about the rules, but that wasn't her. And she prided herself on being staunchly loyal to what she believed in. "But I'd have to withdraw from your case," she whispered as the moment suddenly froze between them.

"Seriously? Over a kiss?"

"I follow the rules, Alain. Always have. And this…this whatever it is won't work because it's not allowed. I can't kid myself over that. It was nice…good…sensational. But I really can't."

"Damn," he grunted out of pure frustration as he stepped back from her. "Leave it to me to find the only girl who's made me want to do that in a long, long time and she's a stickler for the rules."

"I'm sorry," she said, biting her lip to stop the tears that wanted to flow. Because he was the only man who'd ever made her want to break the rules. Break them, throw them out the window, all caution be damned. But that simply wasn't in her makeup. Never had been, never would be. At least, not break the rules and be able to look at herself in the mirror ever again.

"I'm sorry," she said again, this time her voice even more wobbly then before. "I do want to be able to represent you, and I can't do that and... and this. It doesn't work that way for me."

Alain leaned back against the wall and simply shut his eyes. "I think one of the things I like best about you is your ethical principles, but, damn, I never expected it to come back and kick me in the..."

She reached out and took hold of his hand. "It wasn't your fault."

"Because I'm a man and men are expected to be weak in these kinds of situations?"

Maggie laughed. "No. Because I let you down and thought for a few moments that I could have it both ways. For what it's worth, I'm glad you tried."

"For what it's worth, I hate like hell that I failed."

"But getting your life straightened out is more important than anything we might have done here tonight."

Alain let out a jagged sigh. "Just for the record, counselor. Would something more have happened here tonight?"

"I object on the grounds that would be pure speculation." She smiled, kissed her fingertip then brushed it across his lips. "Or I might just have to perjure myself, and you wouldn't want me to do that, would you?"

"Well, then, I suppose court is adjourned."

"For now," she said as she headed for the front door. Then she turned and gave him a serious look. "It was the right thing, Alain. We shouldn't have let it get out of hand and I shouldn't have let it get out of hand. I'm going to have to have a serious talk with Jean-Pierre tomorrow to make sure he wants me to remain on the case, since I did cross the line."

"You think he'll withdraw you?"

"Probably not. Not for one kiss. But I'm going to be treading on thin ice."

"Call me when you know."

She nodded, then disappeared out the door, leaving Alain so disappointed and frustrated that he kicked a hole through the drywall in the newly walled hallway. "Of all the stupid things…"

Yes, he knew her principles. Yes, he even respected them. But nowhere…*nowhere* in that addled brain of his had he thought he'd be the one to step over her line.

He had now, and tomorrow he'd know the consequences. "Damn it to hell," he muttered as he plopped down on his cot and stared up at the ceiling for the next hour, berating himself until he finally fell asleep.

CHAPTER NINE

THREE DAYS LATER on the plane to Illinois was the next time they actually spoke. Maggie had texted him that she had squared the situation with Jean-Pierre, and she'd ignored his text back where he asked about getting together over dinner to talk about the particulars of their case before they left for Illinois. Even on the plane they didn't talk, because they sat distanced by half a plane. Had she purposely booked seats so far apart?

His guess was yes, and when he'd asked her about it in the cab, she simply said that was the way it had worked out. From then on, she was all business, talking about his legal case, maintaining a very hard defining line between them.

So he went along with it. What else was there to do? She was setting the rules and he had no other choice but to follow them. Like Amos and Eula and their unspoken set of rules…rules that had kept them apart for half a lifetime.

"Do I get to talk to Mrs. Gaines when I'm there?" he asked her. "Because I'd like to know why she's choosing me to sue. And I'd also like to find out why her doctor didn't bother to come in for the delivery and pushed it off on me. Did he know about her wish not to have a scar and was that his way to avoid a lawsuit against him? That her pelvis was too narrow for a regular delivery?"

Maggie smiled. "I have an appointment first off with Dr. Green to ask him the same question. I have a hunch we both know the answer to that one, but I'd like to see him squirm a little, and also see how much he's lawyered up. See if I can fight my way into getting you off the hook."

"You really think he'll be there with an attorney?"

"If he's smart, he will be. Anyway, I've also got to meet with Lana Andrews, who's the counsel on record to represent us here. I've already talked to her, and she's going to be on hand if I need some help, but chances are I won't. Her law firm has a reciprocal relationship with ours, so if this thing actually does go to trial, Jean-Pierre will be the one to represent you. But for this little fishing expedition, which is all it is, Lana's going to appear as our attorney of record." She chuckled. "Unless I land a whopper of a deal, which I just may do."

"A whopper?"

"Come and watch me work, Alain. See what I do, and maybe you'll understand better why I have to do it."

"In other words, seeing is believing?"

"It is. And I'm pretty sure you will."

The meeting with Dr. Green was short and not so sweet. He'd lawyered up, as Maggie had expected, and the only thing she was told was that if this matter went to trial, the only way his client would appear was under subpoena, and even then there was the doctor-patient confidentiality agreement, which would be honored. But Maggie hit him with a doozy of a question then watched his face for his answer. "Did she threaten to sue you if you left a scar and is that why she ended up with my client?"

Naturally, he refused to answer, but they said one picture was worth a thousand words, and they'd hit the mark with Dr. Green. Which gave Maggie all the ammunition she needed.

Lana Andrews, the next person they met, as it turned out, was a tiny older woman. Gray hair pulled back in a bun, no-nonsense handshake, stern scowl. Not very formidable looking, to be honest, but Alain was beginning to understand that looks had nothing to do with skill. Lana had the reputation of being a shark, Maggie told him, but a very nice shark, Alain soon discovered as she went over her stipulations for representation.

She was going to allow Maggie to take the lead, and her only part would be to jump in when legalities were close to the edge, or when Maggie was being challenged. "Since this is an informal Q&A and nothing more, I don't expect to take part unless I have to. Oh, but I'd like to have Dr. Lalonde present at the table, and not in the hall. I know that's not what they're going to want to do, but if his presence makes their client so nervous, that tells us more than they want us to know. And I do like to see them squirm."

Maggie laughed, and whispered to Alain as they entered the room en masse, "She's as formidable as Jean-Pierre. I'd hate to see them go head to head."

Admittedly, Alain was the one who was nervous. This was his butt on the line here. Maggie assured him they'd persuade the hospital that they couldn't drop malpractice coverage on him as he'd been employed at the time of the incident, but that was yet another legal action he'd have to endure.

It seemed like all the legalities were just piling up on him and all he could do was stand back and hope that Jean-Pierre, Maggie and now Lana were as good as he thought they were. It was an ugly mess over a simple scar and a beautiful child, and it seemed like such a waste. Ego. Greed.

"We've decided that since these proceedings are about our client, Dr. Lalonde, he should have the right to sit in on them," Lana announced, even before Alain and Maggie were all the way into the room. "And I'm sure you find no objection to that since you believe, in all sincerity, that your client was the wronged party."

"But we stipulated—" John Butterworth, opposing counsel, began.

"Duly noted," Lana said, "but, like I said, the accused has the right to confront his accuser, and doing it here, informally, seems much easier for your client than letting them go at each other for the first time in court. Which, I promise, will make for a very uncomfortable situation." She smiled sweetly, then went in for the kill. *Very uncomfortable.*

Butterworth, a pudgy red-haired man with freckles, dressed in an impeccable hand-tailored blue suit, conferred with his client for a moment while Lana took her place at one side of the table, seated Alain next to her and gestured for Maggie to take her seat in the power position at the end.

"This is always the fun part," Lana whispered to Alain. "Where you can visibly see that you've shaken them up. Good luck, by the way. Jean-Pierre stands behind you, otherwise you would have had one of my junior associates." She gave his arm a squeeze, then sat back in the chair to observe the proceedings.

"Mrs. Gaines has agreed to allow Dr. Lalonde to sit in on the stipulation that as you will be questioning her, we will be allowed to do the same with him."

"Feel free to question away," Maggie said. She spread her notes out in front of her and clearly looked like the person in charge of the room. "But be advised that my client may or may not answer, depending on how his answer could affect the outcome of the end proceedings."

Alain blinked hard. Maggie was in command of everything. Not just her team, but she had it all over the opposition, and the interesting thing was he didn't believe that the opposition was even aware of it.

Alain was impressed. Truly impressed. And for the first time he really thought he understood her. Not all of her but the parts he'd never seen before. This was who Maggie was. Who she was meant to be. Who she had to be. In defense of the doctor... That was her. Nothing there made him doubt that.

But nothing made him regret that kiss, either. And he still believed she could divide herself and be the belle of the ball as well as master of the courtroom. If she wanted to. Question was, did she want to?

"So, as I called this meeting, I'll be the one to start the questioning, and I'd like to keep this brief, if you don't mind."

"We have no objections," Butterworth said.

"First, Mrs. Gaines, I don't see your husband

here with you today. I'd requested him to be present. I hope he's not ill."

"He's fine," she said. "Just…working. Couldn't afford to take the time off."

"I understand," Maggie said, folding her hands on the table in front of her. "Today is his weekly golf game with the heads of several corporations, and I can imagine how important that is."

"It is very important to our corporation," Mrs. Gaines said defensively. "You have no idea."

"No, I can't say that I do. Which leads me to my first question. Why, when Dr. Green had already advised you of the likelihood of having a C-section, are you suing my client?"

"I had specifically stated that I wanted no scars. Your client scarred me."

"Let me make you aware that I talked to Dr. Green just an hour ago. Isn't it true that he warned you of the likelihood of a C-section?" In reality Green had said nothing of the kind. This was only the first part of her fishing expedition.

"You don't have to answer that," Butterworth advised.

"And didn't he describe the kind of scar it might leave?

"Again, don't answer," Butterworth went on.

"And isn't it true that you threatened to sue Dr. Green if he left a scar?"

"Again, I'll advise my client not to answer!"

"You threatened to sue even though Dr. Green advised you there was no other choice?"

"There are always choices!" Mrs. Gaines snapped. "And even though my former doctor, Dr. Green, couldn't seem to find one, Dr. Lalonde worked with high-risk pregnancies and he should have known what to do."

"You mean deliver a healthy baby?" Maggie asked.

"I *said* no scar!"

"Your baby was in fetal distress. Labor was progressing too long."

"But it could have gone on longer. The baby was in the birth canal."

"In danger of dying." For effect, Maggie leaned forward in her chair. "Did that matter to you?"

"Yes, of course it did, but we could have tried a while longer."

"And in Dr. Lalonde's opinion, that was too risky."

"It was only his opinion. I had an opinion, too."

"And a medical degree in high-risk obstetrics to back it up, Mrs. Gaines?"

The woman was beginning to look distressed. "Aren't doctors supposed to do what the patient tells them?"

"Your baby was not going to be delivered alive, Mrs. Gaines. That's the bottom line, and I have affidavits from everyone in the delivery room stating that he tried everything possible to deliver that child naturally, but it wasn't going to happen." Maggie took a deep breath. "So let me ask you this question. What was more important to you? Your scar or your son?"

"That's a despicable question," John Butterworth interjected. "My client's only contending that your client didn't explore all his avenues."

"Her doctor passed off the delivery to whomever was on staff because he didn't want to get sued," Maggie continued. "He knew it was going to be a tough delivery most likely ending in a C-section, and he didn't want to get sued. But your client also knew the odds that she wouldn't be able to deliver naturally, and I have statements from three other obstetricians she visited who will testify to the same thing.

"She suffers from a condition called cephalopelvic disproportion, which means a baby's head will be too large to pass through the pelvic opening. It resulted from a traffic accident in her late teens where her pelvis was fractured. She was aware of the condition and aware of the outcome of any attempted pregnancy."

It was obvious Butterworth had been caught completely off guard. "Your, um...your client didn't try hard enough for a regular delivery. He was with my client only thirty minutes when he made the decision to do a C-section."

Mrs. Gaines sat straight in her chair, her hands folded on the table, looking quite the ice queen. "And my pelvic injury is not the problem here. It healed nicely."

"You're forty-two years old, Mrs. Gaines," Maggie countered. "At least, that's what you claim, even though I've found records showing you are forty-six. Whatever the case, this was your first delivery, which was destined to be difficult due to your condition, and you knew that going in. I'm sorry a C-section scar marred your perfect body, but you have a perfect son as a result.

"Now, here's what I'd like. You knew the risks, you knew the eventual outcome, knew you were likely to have a C-section no matter who delivered your baby. You drop your charges against my client, and we won't take action against you for a wrongful lawsuit. In other words, we'll keep all your dirty little secrets out of court.

Because, trust me, if we go forward from here, you won't have any secrets. Which could affect your husband's golf game, I'm sure."

"We have a right to our day in court, Miss Doucet," Butterworth interjected.

"And your day in court will be spent going up against Jean-Pierre Robichaud. I'm sure you know who he is. He'll win this one easily, Mr. Butterworth. I assure you, you will not stand a chance."

Butterworth conferred with his client for a minute, then said, "For the sake of her son, Mrs. Gaines has opted not to continue with this lawsuit. Consider it dropped."

"And what about Dr. Green?" Alain asked.

"He's a victim, like you are. So I don't think we should pursue him."

"And the hospital?" Alain asked.

Maggie smiled. "Lana's agreed to fix that mess, pro bono."

"Then it's over?"

Maggie nodded. "Most of it is. We still need

to convince the hospital to confess the error of its ways and make that right."

"And I can kiss you?"

"Circumspectly, as this is a legal chamber."

But the kiss he gave her was anything but circumspect, and Lana simply smiled at them as she walked out the door and shut it behind her.

Maggie and Alain greeted each other with a cordial embrace three days later. Except for a friendly parting at the airport, they'd had no contact, and he'd wondered if that was because he was pushing her too hard. Women who kissed back the way Maggie had that day after the hearing had feelings, and maybe she just didn't want to confront them, or didn't know how. Whatever the case, he'd decided to give her the space she wanted then see what might happen in due course, when she was feeling comfortable again.

God only knew how anxious he was to see her, to kiss her or even just talk to her. But Maggie was making it quite clear that they were on her terms now. She took his calls but cut them short, texted him back with brief one- or two-word answers and refused pizza with him and Lilly.

Which meant she was seriously resisting him now that the case was over.

The thing was, he didn't know what to do about that because he wanted Maggie in his life not just for himself but also for Lilly, who missed her and moped around without her. Wouldn't even wear her pink shoes to pizza because Maggie wasn't coming.

"What have I done?" he asked himself as he sat on the porch one afternoon and watched Lilly sulking around in the play yard while two of her little friends played there with her and seemed to be having a good time. Lilly, who'd finally been coming out of her shell, thanks largely to Maggie, was now in full retreat again, and he felt bad about it. Felt bad about everything.

"She can be had," Amos Picou said as he settled in across from Alain. "Just not in the way you're used to."

"I don't want to just have her," Alain snapped.

Amos let out a low whistle then laughed. "You got it bad, and that ain't good. Mellette and Justin were easy to get together because they both knew what they wanted. Had a few rough patches to fix up, but true love always wins."

"The difference is they loved each other."

"And you and Maggie don't?"

"It's not that simple."

"Love is never that simple. It's not meant to be, or else you'd be falling in love with every girl who ever crossed your path."

"Well, one did cross my path, but she doesn't want to have anything to do with falling in love or having a relationship. Which means she doesn't want anything to do with me."

"Do you think she loves you?"

"She might. For a few days I deluded myself into thinking she did."

"And do you love her?"

"Against my better judgment, yes. Didn't mean to, especially since she's such a challenge. But it happened."

"Then you just go get her."

"Sure. I'll go all caveman, force my way into her office, throw her over my shoulder and carry her out."

"If that's what it takes. Because sitting here complaining to me sure won't do it."

"Says the man who never went out and got the woman he loved," Alain snapped, then immediately regretted his words. "Look, I'm sorry. I shouldn't have said that. But I'm so damned frustrated I don't know what to do."

"You don't do what I did, which was spend a lifetime wishing, without ever telling her."

Alain looked up at the sign over the door. "Eula's House," he said aloud. "From what I understand, it's come a long way."

"Folks in these parts weren't so trusting at first. Kind of like your Maggie. But they're settling in to the idea of having a legitimate practice here. We still like our herbs, and that's not going to change. It's not right, going against the general nature of things. But compromising is good, and that's what we're doing here with Eula's House." He smiled. "Compromise is a mighty powerful thing if you do it right."

"But Maggie's not willing to listen to a compromise."

"You're sure of that?"

Alain thought for a moment. Then smiled. "I don't suppose I'm really open to one, either. My idea is to get my life back on track and go back to work the way I used to."

"Which was what?"

"Ten or twelve hours a day."

"Leaving how much time for Maggie, who'll be working that much, too, if you were so lucky as to reel her in?"

"Leaving not much. And I've been thinking about adopting Lilly, as well."

"Ah, see, the plot thickens. You and Maggie want the same things, only differently. Truth is, to get what you want, you've got to be willing to give up what you want, as well." Amos rose from his seat and headed off the porch. "You're not going to get twelve hours a day at work, a wife and a child. Won't happen, Alain, so don't delude yourself. Change that plan of yours and maybe that woman might see fit to change that plan of hers. At least it gives you something to talk about."

"Easier said than done," he muttered as Amos walked away.

"I've got mighty good hearing for a man of my years, son. And if you want that woman, you'd better make it easier done than said." With that, he laughed and disappeared down the trail.

"I can take the house call," Maggie said three hours later as she sat her medical bag on the table in exam one. "You can stay here with Lilly."

"Lilly's really missed you. She won't even wear her pink shoes. You sure you don't mind staying here with her while I run out and check on Zerelda's bronchitis?"

"I'd love to stay with Lilly. I've missed her. But remember that Zerelda prefers a decoction of colt's foot."

"That, and a good antihistamine."

Maggie shook her head. "Colt's foot. She won't stand for anything else."

"I know, but I always live in hope."

"If it works, it works. Anyway, tell her I said hello and that I'll stop by and see her in a day or two." With that, Maggie flitted out to the play yard in a way that almost seemed like she was brushing him off. Certainly, her friendliness was superficial. Nothing substantial about it, the way it used to be. And here Amos thought all he had to do was tell her how he felt then start making compromises. The only way Maggie would react to that was to run away entirely.

"So get over her," he said as he climbed into the truck and headed down an overgrown path to see Zerelda Lavache and give her the herb of her choice.

* * *

No one had made an appointment, and the knock on the front door wasn't unexpected, as people stopped by all the time. But this knock was loud, abrasive, angry, and Maggie's first instinct was to tell Lilly to run upstairs and play in the bedroom. She wasn't sure why she did it, but that was what her gut was telling her to do, and it was exactly what she did.

By the time Lilly was safely out of the way, the person outside had banged twice more, each time louder. So she approached the door cautiously and looked out and saw someone standing on the porch with a hand wrapped up in a bloody towel.

Normally, they kept the door locked and people were used to knocking, so this was nothing new, but when Maggie saw the potential injury she threw open the door and was immediately shoved back into the room, where she hit her head on the opposite wall. As it turned out, the bloody towel was a ruse. The man charging the door was as fit as anybody she'd ever encountered.

"Where is she?" the man shouted. He seemed vaguely familiar.

"What?" she said, trying to pull herself upright. But as soon as she'd pulled herself partway up, he shoved her flat onto the floor again, so hard she found herself fighting to breathe again. She opened her eyes enough to see him tearing up the office, knocking over chairs, breaking windows… It was the man from whom they'd taken Lilly. Joe Aucoin.

Dear God! He was here to take her back.

"Where is she?" he screamed when he realized Maggie's eyes were following him around the room.

"House call with the doctor," she lied, praying to God that Lilly had heard the noise and hidden herself somewhere.

"I don't believe you. Tell me where she is."

He went into the kitchen, which gave her enough time to push herself up to her hands and knees and look for a weapon…anything. But there was nothing there that would hurt him or incapacitate him. Everything she could see would only make him even angrier, so her only alternative was to get upstairs to Lilly and see if there was any way they could hide or even get out of the house.

Even though she was injured, Maggie pushed herself all the way up and made a mad dash for the stairs. Got up them and into the room where Lilly was. Found Lilly under the bed, trembling.

Lilly immediately started sobbing the instant she saw Maggie, and Maggie shushed her with a finger to her lips. "We've got to get out of here," she whispered to the girl, "so when I tell you to run, I want you to run as hard and fast as you can down the stairs and don't stop until you get to Amos Picou's house. Do you understand me?"

Lilly swiped at the tears running down her face, and nodded.

"Then tell Amos I need help. That your uncle is after me. Can you do that for me, Lilly?"

Lilly nodded.

What Maggie didn't want to say was that Lilly's uncle wanted to kill her, and that was what she feared he'd do. "Okay, now I'm going to call…" She reached into her pocket only to discover that her cell phone must have fallen out during the altercation. "I'm going to go through to the next bedroom and make some noise, Lilly. Your uncle will hear it and come upstairs. As soon as he gets in the room where I am, I want you to run. Please, run, Lilly! As hard and fast as you ever have."

"Will you come?" Lilly asked.

"In a while. But I've got to make sure you get away from him first. Okay? Now, be brave. And run hard, Lilly."

"I love you, Maggie."

"And I love you, too, sweetheart." And she did, truly. Like a mother would, she suddenly discovered, because she knew she would literally give her life to save this child. "Now get ready." Maggie pulled away from the bed and made her way quietly down the hall. Found a glass table lamp that might stun her attacker, grabbed it and purposely knocked a figurine onto the floor, then dived under the bed.

Instantly she heard thundering footsteps on their way upstairs, and she prayed that Lilly wasn't too afraid to do what needed to be done. Otherwise there was no telling what would happen to either of them.

"Where the hell are you?" he screamed. "I know you're up here, so show yourself so we can talk."

He stomped very slowly down the hall. Too slowly, and Maggie heard him stop at Lilly's bedroom for an instant. Her stomach churned and she retched involuntarily. Which was all Joe Aucoin needed to find her huddled under the bed in the back bedroom.

"I know where you're hiding!" he screamed at her. "Won't do you no good, 'cause I got you now." He grabbed hold of her left ankle and started to pull her out from under the bed, but she fought him. And when she realized she wasn't going to win this battle, she latched on to the nightstand lamp and pulled it along with her, hoping that somewhere in all this she might just have one element of surprise.

But that wasn't to be the case, because he picked her up as easily as if she were a rag doll, then threw her on the bed and pinned here there. "We can do this the easy way, or it can get ugly," he said.

"She's not here," Maggie said, trying to extricate herself from underneath his weight. "She's with the doctor, so you'd better get out of here before he returns."

His response was to laugh. "I saw the doctor leave, and he wasn't dragging the brat along with him, so you've got her hidden. All you've got to do is give me what's mine and I'll be done with you."

Maggie didn't say anything. There was no point in provoking the man any more than she already had. So she went limp, shut her eyes, stayed limp when he yanked her up off the bed and started shaking her. "Give her to me now!" he bellowed, even though Maggie was feigning unconsciousness.

"Leave her alone!" a tiny voice screamed.

Maggie opened her eyes just in time to see Lilly run across the floor, make a lunge for Joe Aucoin and grab hold of his leg. In that instant he dropped Maggie and she immediately grabbed the table lamp and came right back up, swinging. Hit him in the head, left shards of glass everywhere, even though the hit only stunned him, caused him to start swinging blindly as blood dripped into his eyes. And his target...Lilly. He hit her and knocked her down to the floor, then immediately picked her up and started to run out the door with her.

But Maggie flew after him, grabbed hold of him from behind before he got to the stairs. His only reaction was to swing round and kick her so she fell backward and couldn't get up. Still, she crawled over to the steps, pulled herself up on the banister and forced herself to remain standing as the man made his way down with the child in his arms.

"No!" Maggie screamed. "You can't take her."

"She's right," Alain said, appearing at the bottom of the steps. He was holding a walking stick, no other weapon. And his form filled the entire opening, dwarfing Joe Aucoin. "Put the child down and walk away."

Maggie dragged herself down the steps, one by one, until she was standing directly behind the man. Her immediate action was to pound him directly on the back, and as he spun to take a swing at her, Alain lunged forward and grabbed Lilly away from him. Then he set her on a chair out of the way of the fighting and went back in with his walking stick and took a crack at Joe Aucoin's face, then another one at his chest. It was enough to bring the man to his knees and cause him to topple onto the floor at the bottom of the steps.

Maggie immediately threw herself over the

man to keep him from getting back up while Alain went to get rope to tie him. But as he did so he noticed that Lilly was slumped over in the chair, her pallor the color of paste. So he tossed Maggie the rope and immediately began to assess the child. "Broken ribs," he shouted, as Maggie tied the man up in several knots of her own making. "Probably from the way he was carrying her. I think she might have a pneumothorax." Punctured lung. "She's struggling to breathe."

Immediately, Maggie went to Alain's medical bag and found an eighteen-gauge needle and attached it to a syringe. He listened to her chest through his stethoscope, an over the top of one of the ribs in the area where there were no breath sounds. The reason it was over-the-top and no deeper was to avoid a nerve, artery and veins that ran underneath each rib.

As soon as Alain found the spot, he inserted the needle and pulled back on the syringe. Immediately he started pulling back air, which was where he stopped, as if he'd gone any farther he could have stuck the lung and made the condition worse. "Do you know how many years it's been since I've had to do that?" he asked, wiping the sweat off his face with the back of his hand. He glanced over at Aucoin, who was squirming around on the floor like the worm that he was.

"I've called the authorities to come and get him, and a helicopter is en route to get Lilly, so we need to get her over to Grandmaison, where they'll meet her."

"Looks as though you've taken a few good licks yourself," he said as he bundled Lilly up in a blanket and got ready to take her to the truck.

"A few, nothing serious."

"You sure?"

She nodded. "I was just so…so scared for Lilly."

"She's going to be fine, Maggie. Once we get her to the hospital…"

Because Maggie had taken a beating herself, it was decided she'd fly in by helicopter and meet her entire family, who'd be waiting for her in Emergency. Since she felt like death warmed over, she didn't object, but she sure wished there'd been room to accommodate Alain, too. Because she didn't want him to let her go as he carried her to the helicopter. But they had to part, and he left her with a tender kiss. "One more?" she asked before he backed away.

Alain laughed. But obliged. One more kiss, and then the woman he loved was lifted into the clear nighttime sky.

CHAPTER TEN

"YOU LOOK AS if you've been through a battle," Alain said as Maggie reached up and ran her fingers over the bandage on her head, slightly above her left eye. She was wearing a lovely pale blue cotton hospital gown that would make even the most robust person look sick, and she was lucky enough that her name afforded her a private room so no one would have to see her looking like that unless she wanted them to.

Like Alain... If ever she wanted someone to see her when she wasn't at her best, he was the one. He'd been with Lilly, and she knew that, but she'd waited hours for him to find a minute or two for her.

"Just a small one. No big deal. But how's Lilly? I keep getting reports from various members of my family, but I want to hear it from you."

He brushed his thumb over her cheek. "Lilly's fine now, and she's resting comfortably in the pediatric intensive care. Asking for you, by the way. She's worried her uncle might have hurt you."

"I'll dab on some makeup in a little while and go down to see her. And Joe Aucoin? What happened to him?"

"From what I heard, Gertrude Aucoin was smiling when the authorities carted off her husband."

"Does she want Lilly back now?"

Alain shook his head. "She's going to Mississippi to live with her cousin. Said she's packed her bag, and that's all she's going to take with her."

"Which means…?"

"Lilly's officially abandoned now."

"Which is good for her?"

"Maybe good for me, too. The court is going to leave her with me for the time being until she's over the trauma."

"How long have I been sleeping?"

"Why?"

"I've missed so much."

"Eighteen hours."

"Seriously? I've slept for eighteen hours?"

Alain nodded as he took hold of her hand. "With the help of some medication. You were exhausted. Your doctor decided you needed some time to rest."

"My doctor?"

"Sabine Doucet."

Maggie smiled and sighed, and her eyes started to flutter shut. "She's good."

"So are you, Maggie. You saved Lilly's life."

"All I remember for sure was a kiss."

"Like this?" he asked as he touched his lips gently to hers.

"So nice…" she murmured, as she faded out.

It was two more days before Maggie was released from the hospital, and she was only released because she was going to have round-the-clock medical care at home. For the first day her whole family hovered around her, treating her like a fine piece of porcelain.

Alain, who was spending most of his time at the hospital with Lilly, did manage to find time to stop in and check on her, but he nearly had to stand in line to do so. On the third day, though, when Maggie was up and about on her own, everyone left the two of them alone.

"I've got good news for you," he said as they sat together on the veranda and he gave her a circumspect kiss on the cheek, which had turned into their custom when any of the other Doucet family was lurking nearby. Or, in this case, just inside the house, probably peeking out of the window.

"Lilly's mine, if I want to adopt her."

"That's great news!" Maggie exclaimed. "I'm happy for you." She paused for a moment, saw the concerned look on his face. "So what's the problem?"

"Frankly, you are. You and I have barely

started something, and it's something I don't want to give up on. But I don't know where we stand now, and I don't know how you feel about starting a new life with an instant family."

"I love Lilly," she confessed.

"Just Lilly?"

"I love you, too. And I don't mind if it's a package deal."

"You won't be getting much from me in the way of worldly goods. At least, not for a while."

"I don't need worldly goods."

"And the mansion is a long way off from being ready to live in comfortably."

"I don't mind roughing it."

"And I'm going to be working a lot of hours between all my jobs, because your mother's offered me a position at New Hope in Obstetrics—I'm going to head up the high-risk cases. Plus I've got work to do at Eula's House to get it finished, because I promised, and I don't break promises."

"So are you proposing to me or backing out?" Maggie asked.

"Just letting you know what's entailed."

"When you get mixed up in the Doucet family, everything's entailed," she said, reaching over to take his hand.

"I sort of figured that out while you were in the hospital. They whooshed in en masse and took over."

Maggie smiled. "So are you up to it?"

"They don't scare me."

"Especially when you become one of them."

"Is that a yes?"

"A definite yes to you, to Lilly and to us as a family. Oh, and all the malpractice charges against you have been dropped and Jean-Pierre has a nice settlement check waiting for you from the hospital. After all the glowing publicity from what happened here, plus your war record, no one was about to go up against you. So you win…everything."

"Then allow me one thing to make this right

with your family." He got up from the swing and steadied it, then went down on one knee. "Magnolia Loraine Doucet, will you marry me?"

Inside the house the curtains parted.

"Yes," she said quietly as he placed a large diamond-and-emerald ring on her finger. It had been his grandmother's ring, held ready for him until the time he proposed. "Yes," she said again, only this time loud enough for everyone inside to hear.

Then cheers erupted.

But Alain and Maggie didn't hear them, for they were already locked in a kiss that carried them far, far beyond the Doucet front porch to a place where only the two of them existed.

* * * * *

MILLS & BOON®
Large Print Medical

February

TEMPTED BY HER BOSS	Scarlet Wilson
HIS GIRL FROM NOWHERE	Tina Beckett
FALLING FOR DR DIMITRIOU	Anne Fraser
RETURN OF DR IRRESISTIBLE	Amalie Berlin
DARING TO DATE HER BOSS	Joanna Neil
A DOCTOR TO HEAL HER HEART	Annie Claydon

March

A SECRET SHARED...	Marion Lennox
FLIRTING WITH THE DOC OF HER DREAMS	Janice Lynn
THE DOCTOR WHO MADE HER LOVE AGAIN	Susan Carlisle
THE MAVERICK WHO RULED HER HEART	Susan Carlisle
AFTER ONE FORBIDDEN NIGHT...	Amber McKenzie
DR PERFECT ON HER DOORSTEP	Lucy Clark

April

IT STARTED WITH NO STRINGS…	Kate Hardy
ONE MORE NIGHT WITH HER DESERT PRINCE…	Jennifer Taylor
FLIRTING WITH DR OFF-LIMITS	Robin Gianna
FROM FLING TO FOREVER	Avril Tremayne
DARE SHE DATE AGAIN?	Amy Ruttan
THE SURGEON'S CHRISTMAS WISH	Annie O'Neil

MILLS & BOON®
Large Print Medical

May

PLAYING THE PLAYBOY'S SWEETHEART	Carol Marinelli
UNWRAPPING HER ITALIAN DOC	Carol Marinelli
A DOCTOR BY DAY...	Emily Forbes
TAMED BY THE RENEGADE	Emily Forbes
A LITTLE CHRISTMAS MAGIC	Alison Roberts
CHRISTMAS WITH THE MAVERICK MILLIONAIRE	Scarlet Wilson

June

MIDWIFE'S CHRISTMAS PROPOSAL	Fiona McArthur
MIDWIFE'S MISTLETOE BABY	Fiona McArthur
A BABY ON HER CHRISTMAS LIST	Louisa George
A FAMILY THIS CHRISTMAS	Sue MacKay
FALLING FOR DR DECEMBER	Susanne Hampton
SNOWBOUND WITH THE SURGEON	Annie Claydon

July

HOW TO FIND A MAN IN FIVE DATES	Tina Beckett
BREAKING HER NO-DATING RULE	Amalie Berlin
IT HAPPENED ONE NIGHT SHIFT	Amy Andrews
TAMED BY HER ARMY DOC'S TOUCH	Lucy Ryder
A CHILD TO BIND THEM	Lucy Clark
THE BABY THAT CHANGED HER LIFE	Louisa Heaton